OWEN G. IRONS

THE TRAIL TO TRINITY

Complete and Unabridged

LINFORD
Leicester

First published in Great Britain in 2015 by
Robert Hale Limited
London

First Linford Edition
published 2018
by arrangement with
Robert Hale
an imprint of The Crowood Press
Wiltshire

A catalogue record for this book is available
from the British Library.

ISBN 978–1–4448–3661–5

Published by
F. A. Thorpe (Publishing)
Anstey, Leicestershire

Set by Words & Graphics Ltd.
Anstey, Leicestershire
Printed and bound in Great Britain by
T. J. International Ltd., Padstow, Cornwall

This book is printed on acid-free paper

THE TRAIL TO TRINITY

The Trail to Trinity is rugged, and dangerous as hell. Sage Paxton rides it only out of the direst of necessities — to avenge his murdered parents. Sage has decided that their killer will not see another day. Bad weather, a lame horse, a crooked army officer, and outlaws will not keep him from his prize. Nothing else matters now, not even his own life. Before the end of the day, he will have vengeance against his parents' killer — and his own brother . . .

1

Mesa Verde was off to his right, the town of Tucker behind him. Sage Paxton — for that was the lone rider's name — could see neither of them through the hammering sheets of wind-driven rain, nor was he looking for them. He did give occasional thought to the town of Tucker, barely remembering a thing about the squat little collection of faded buildings but the warmth and comfort of the dry bed he had occupied only the night before.

Just now Sage was as wet and cold as a man can get. He was draped in his black rain slicker, wearing leather gloves. These were small protection from the elements, did little to keep him warm. Beneath him was a wet saddle, slick and cold. The insides of his legs were damp with water. The rain had built itself up into a kind of fury, lashing his face with an almost personal rage.

Sage knew he should have listened to those who advised him against riding on such a day, to remain where he was, toasty and comfortable in his bed, but he felt the time had passed when he could abide delay or justify his own reluctance to continue on that lonesome trail to Trinity.

The dull-witted kid with the gapped teeth had looked at Sage, looked to the darkening skies outside the stable and shaken his head. 'Mister, you ain't got to go nowhere this bad.' The stable hand was a kid on the poor side of half bright and Sage had shrugged off this advice as he would have almost any comment he had to make. It just went to show Sage that his own daddy had been right when he had told him, 'Son, you can learn something from almost every man.'

For the rain did not pour down, it hammered against Sage's poncho. The sky beasts crackled and roared. When the lightning flared, the land went to a strange yellow-white, when it flickered out the world became a black, feature-less place hung with ozone and battered by a constant, raging wind.

'I ain't got to go nowhere this bad,' Sage muttered to himself.

But he did. The impulse to reach Trinity was irresistible, the drive to reach it as soon as possible like a thrust between his shoulder blades, impelling him onward through the blustering, icy cold of the night.

Then his horse went down.

Sage felt the gray misstep, falter and then its big body seemed to cramp up, and before Sage could pull back on the reins, get the horse's head up, it rolled on him and he was thrown roughly to the sodden black earth. Stunned, soaked through in a few new places, he yet saw by the animal's silhouette that it had struggled to its feet and was standing head down, reins dangling.

'Why, you stupid nag,' Sage said through chattering teeth as he pushed himself to his feet. Then he saw that the gray was standing with none of its weight on its right hind leg in the classic posture of a wounded horse. Sage moved stiffly toward it in the cold shower of the rain.

'What have you done to yourself now?' he breathed. The gray horse winced at even the light touch of Sage's hands on its hock. The tendon was strained if not torn. Sage straightened up and stood, hands on hips. His situation which had been pitiable before now had become desperate.

'Can you hobble on it?' he asked the horse, his words unheard even by himself above the din of the storm. Because they had to keep moving, to find some place to be on this savage and dangerous night. To remain where they were was death.

Gathering the horse's reins, Sage trudged on, carrying the sullen anger that only comes to a man who knows he is responsible for his own troubles.

Sage had some idea of where he

wanted to go, a dimmer notion of the direction he needed to take and little hope of reaching it. Up along the juncture of the Vasquez River and Clabber Creek the army had established a garrison. If he could reach the outpost he could at least find shelter and warmth which were now becoming critical as the temperature dropped and the soaking rain continued to fall. Hat streaming water before his eyes, rain sheeting the ground, the mud thick underfoot, Sage Paxton started in that direction leading his crippled horse with only the occasional sharp beacons of lightning to guide him.

It seemed days, years, although it was actually only four or five slogging hours later that he reached the fort perched on an outcropping above the rain-swollen, madly rushing Vasquez River.

He approached the front gate and shouted out his name and situation above the swish and swirl of the wind and the driving hiss of the rain to a guard in his miserable shelter on the parapet above.

This man yelled something to a second soldier below who apparently was dispatched to ask a third if the infidel at the gates could be admitted. As if, Sage thought sourly, he looked like some sort of assaulting force instead of the miserable, sodden wretch he was.

He knew it was the army way, and he waited patiently, taking some comfort in the way that the log palisades of the fort protected him from the roughest thrusts of the buffeting wind.

After a while he was admitted to the empty interior of the fort. There were no soldiers visible across the yard, no horses. Everyone was a little smarter than he. They were all tucked away, respectively, in their barracks or stables.

'Didn't no one want to wake the captain,' his soldier guide yelled as they crossed the stormy yard. 'The first-shirt said for you to shelter up in the sutler's store if it's still open!' Too weary for answering, Sage only nodded his head.

A dim lantern showed in the oilskin-covered window of what he took to be the sutler's store, since that was their announced destination. A man in civilian clothes appeared briefly on the covered plank walk before the store, looked up and down, shook his head and went back inside.

'That's Mr Kiebler — he will take care of you!' the soldier shouted above the storm and then departed for warmer, drier places. Sage nodded again. Whether the man would help him or not, he was already in a better place. If he had to sleep outside under the awning, he would. He would be drier, and the heat from the interior of the building could be felt radiating, if only slightly, through the wall. Loosely wrapping the reins of his suffering, put-upon horse around the hitch rail, he went up on to the boardwalk, rapped on the door and waited. The sign on the door had been turned to read 'Closed', but his knock was answered almost immediately by the man, Kiebler, who looked Sage over and took his arm.

'For God's sake, man! See to your horse and then get inside. Didn't your momma ever tell you not to stand around in the rain?'

'She probably did; I probably didn't listen,' Sage answered. When he returned from the stable he was tugged inside to find himself dripping cold water on the wooden floor of the sutler's small store. There was an iron stove in the center of the room and Sage was inexorably drawn to it, shedding his slicker as he went.

'I'll take that,' Kiebler offered. He was a small, pot-bellied man with alert, flickering blue eyes and a hairline which time had pushed far back on the crown of his skull. He hung the slicker on a row of pegs along the wall apparently used for soldiers' coats. Sage stood shivering by the stove, slowly letting the heat seep into his bones.

'Blustery night out,' Kiebler commented, as he returned to the stove to hold his hands over it.

'More like the devil's tangle,' Sage said without a smile.

'Well, then, lucky I wasn't out in it. I've got my safe haven and I mean to stay inside it. Let the younger, wilder men try to best a night like this.' The wind rattled the oilskin coverings on the window and caused the floor to shudder a little. 'You had a reason for being out in it?' Kiebler asked, glancing at Sage Paxton's stove-brightened face.

'I'm riding to kill a man,' Sage answered.

'Must be a killing that can't wait,' Kiebler said, as if the matter had no interest for him. 'I was about to fix myself something to eat now that the soldiers have all been shut down in their barracks. Will you join me, Mr — ?'

'Paxton, Sage Paxton. Yes I'd be happy to have some of whatever you're eating.'

'That remains to be seen,' Kiebler said, lifting his shaggy eyebrows. 'I'm hardly a French chef.

'Paxton . . . it seems like I've heard that name somewhere before.'

'Not from me,' Sage answered with a smile.

'No, no.' Kiebler's face was thoughtful. 'I'll get to my cooking. Would you care for a beer while you wait?'

'I could do that,' Sage answered gratefully. His eyes had been going around the store, seeing the stock on its well-tended shelves, wondering that the sutler kept so many various items there.

'You've sure got yourself a variety of goods,' he said.

'Never enough,' Kiebler said from behind the counter where he had selected a tin of corned beef which he was now opening. 'Stuck out here as they are, these soldiers ache to spend their money on payday. This is the only place they can come to to divest themselves of their army scrip.' Kiebler smiled faintly and returned to the stove with the open tin of corned beef and a frying pan.

'I see you carry tins of peaches,' Sage said.

'Those sell well. To men stuck on an army diet of beef and beans, anything different is special. I also do well with pen and paper, pocket knives, tobacco and beer as you can imagine, and with civilian clothes for those boys who are being discharged and want to wear almost anything that is not army blue.

'Fresh fruit they cannot get enough of — when I can procure it — and potatoes.'

'They buy potatoes from you? On an army post?' Sage asked, not understanding. 'Surely they have those for the soldiers.'

'They do,' Kiebler said, stirring the corned beef. 'Mashed potatoes, boiled potatoes. A lot of the men here tell me that once a potato has been in water it no longer tastes like the potatoes they have known. Those boys — mostly from the South — want whole potatoes they can cook on a stick over an open fire

11

until the skin is black and crusty. I get a nickel apiece for potatoes.'

'A nickel . . .'

'I know,' Kiebler said with a quick smile as he dabbed the corned beef on to two tin plates and brought out a crusty loaf of bread from somewhere. 'Five cents for a potato when I buy them for twenty-five cents a ten-pound sack doesn't seem fair, but whatever a man can't easily get has value. The going rate is a nickel a spud, and I always run out of them before the end of the month.'

'I see — then you were wise in buying the government license for this store.'

'I suppose,' Kiebler said, scratching at his earlobe. 'You know, Paxton, these things always seem like a cushy deal to others once they're done and finalized, but believe me, scraping up the money for the license, calculating the distance between the western forts and whatever suppliers you might have to wrangle with, the delays in shipping, I couldn't recommend it to anyone wishing to get rich quick.'

'Not even at a nickel a spud,' Sage commented, finishing his poor meal.

'Not even at a nickel a spud.' Kiebler rose, taking Sage's dinner plate with him. 'We don't have dessert on the menu,' the storekeeper said.

'I see a lot of candy around,' Sage commented.

'Candy I have. The younger troopers, especially, spend a fair amount of their pay on it. The army doesn't offer dessert with its meals either, not on this post at least. We have no baker and little else. We're on the very fringe of the so-called civilized lands.'

'And the candy's hard for you to come by,' Sage guessed, rising in his wet jeans and sodden shirt.

'You've no idea — seems you're starting to appreciate the difficulty of the business.'

'Enough so that I won't even ask you what you sell that saltwater taffy for.'

Kiebler grinned as Sage let loose a

long-stifled yawn and stretched his cramped arms overhead. The lantern was burning low. The world outside was still in chaos. 'You can make yourself a bed on those empty potato sacks over in the corner,' Kiebler said, indicating a stack of burlap bags. 'I don't suppose the army would like a civilian bunking in the barracks, even if you wanted to go back out into the storm to walk over there and explain yourself.'

'No, I don't suppose so either. The first sergeant directed me over here.' He finished the beer in his bottle. 'What do I owe you for dinner and a drink?' He thrust his hand into the pocket of his wet jeans.

'They're on your tab,' Kiebler answered.

'I can't take any of your goods without payment,' Sage objected.

'I didn't say I wouldn't expect payment,' Kiebler said. Sitting on a stool the old man explained, 'Look, Paxton, you seem to be stuck here for at least a day or two. There's not a horse

14

to be had on an army post, as you know, and your own mount doesn't appear up to even walking across the parade ground. You've got to let it heal up before you travel on.

'In the meantime, if you'll agree, I could use your help on a short run I have to make up to Barlow, a little place up in the hills not far from here. A man named Mackay grows apples and cherries, and he being so far from markets, I can cut a fair deal with him for his produce. I don't know how he made any money before the fort was built.'

'Can't he bring his apples down and sell them directly to the soldiers?'

'No, he can't. My warrant gives me exclusive rights to such commerce.'

'Mackay doesn't object to that arrangement?'

'Wouldn't do him much good if he did. The army's strict about matters like that — outside purveyors — it keeps things like bad whiskey from making their way on to the post, anything else that might be considered harmful. This way if a soldier gets sick from anything there's only one man to look at — me.'

'And you don't provide whiskey?'

'I do not. It's so stipulated in my warrant. I've posted a copy of it on the wall over there so that I can refer any trooper who wants me to do a little smuggling that the subject is taboo. It would ruin me to be caught dealing in whiskey, stolen goods, shoddy merchandise of any kind, and I won't.

'No, Paxton, Mackay can't do business with anyone but me, and he's happy to do it. We both make a fair profit the way things are arranged.

'Now, get some rest. I'm going to be turning the lantern out. Tomorrow I'll expect you to be helping me load sacks of apples and boxes of cherries up at Mackay's farm. Don't look so glum, Paxton. Look at it this way: this man you want to kill, whoever it is, will not have gotten away during this storm. By the time you reach Trinity, he should be waiting for you still . . . unless someone else has already done the job for you, and then there's no need to rush at all.'

Sage spread the empty potato sacks in the corner until he had a good-enough bed. Stripping off his wet outer clothes he lay down, grateful for the lingering warmth the dying fire in the iron stove emitted. Sometime later he heard Kiebler approach his bed and throw a blanket over him, and Sage closed his eyes as the storm continued to fuss and bluster beyond the flimsy walls of the store.

The stove still glowed a deep cherry red when Sage, unable to sleep, sat up in his rough bed sometime later and rubbed at his head vigorously. Why had he agreed to help Kiebler? Well, because the man had done him some favors and what the sutler said about Sage's horse not being able to travel on just then was quite true.

Also true was the fact that his quarry was likely to have remained in Trinity and not braved the storm to run away. No, he would be there, unless as

Kiebler had said someone else had already done the job for him.

But that would not do, Sage thought, as he again rolled into his bed, pulling his blanket tightly around him. It would not do at all to have someone else kill the man. It had to be Sage, and it had to be face to face.

The wind rattled in the reaches of the little building and the night temperature dropped still more. Sage was able to fall off to sleep this time, warmed by the inner glow of his impending revenge.

2

They were on their way to Mackay's farm by the time the first light had begun to shine through the remnant broken clouds the storm had left in its passing. They had made their departure before the fort was awake, Kiebler believing that a stealthy departure had the advantage over lingering to explain matters to the company commander.

The little storekeeper had also bargained with the corporal in charge of the stable to keep Sage's gray horse warm, fed and doctored if possible. There was a heavy bribe involved in this agreement. Three sheets of saltwater taffy.

Now as the land rose, Kiebler continued to guide his two-horse team easily, almost aimlessly it seemed to Sage. He did not know the trail — if this track winding through the barren oak trees and shuddering pines could be called that.

'It'll be a while,' Kiebler told him. 'You might as well doze and dream of this hot urge for revenge you're carrying around.'

'You mention that lightly, as if it were a small matter,' Sage said with some testiness.

'Well, I know it isn't to you. But how can it be so important that you are risking your own well-being, playing tag with death over something that probably only has importance to you?'

'You don't understand at all,' Sage said bitterly, shifting in his seat.

'No,' Kiebler said after a while. 'I don't. I'll listen if you want to talk about it, but I can't promise that I'll understand the rush of a young man toward death no matter what you have to say.'

'It's my brother I'm after,' Sage said.

'Then perhaps your revenge should be tempered a little with mercy, given the family connection,' Kiebler, who

20

had produced a pipe and lighted it, observed.

Sage's voice was nearly savage as he answered, 'It was my mother and father he killed.'

To that there was no response the good-natured Kiebler could make. Sage was seething inside with the need to repay a blood debt, and the storekeeper could see that there was no way anyone would talk Sage out of his mission.

Kiebler fell silent and continued to guide his team up the slope toward Mackay's secluded farm. 'That over there is Barlow,' the sutler did say a mile or so on, and Sage looking that way saw a dozen shanties huddled together on a dust-colored meadow.

'It's not much to look at.'

'It's even less to visit. The view you get from here is the best you'll get of the town.'

'It's of no nevermind to me — I don't plan on ever seeing it again.'

'I can't say it would enrich your life any,' Kiebler said with a sort of snort which might have been caused by inhaling tobacco smoke.

'How far is Mackay's place?' Sage asked.

'Not far. What does it matter to you? You've the time to waste. Your horse won't have gotten better overnight.'

'No, I know it. Why couldn't I have landed some place where I could trade it?'

'It was your decision to come to Fort Vasquez. It could be that you've been making a lot of rash decisions these days.'

'Could be,' Sage admitted. Then he fell into a studied silence.

As the land rose higher, the pines grew more densely. The sky was holding blue, stained only by a few scattered, drifting clouds.

'There 'tis,' Kiebler said, holding the team up at the crest of the timbered knoll they were travelling, and Sage lifted his eyes to see the meadow below them, situated prettily among the surrounding pine-clad hills beside a slowly moving, sinuous stream. There was about an acre of apple trees behind the house, some barren, and to one side stood a smaller orchard. From what Kiebler had told Sage, he assumed them to be cherry trees, although he could not identify them without their blossoms which were long gone at this time of year.

'The man's got himself a nice-looking place,' Sage commented.

'Yes, if he were any nearer to a town, he'd be doing all right.'

'What about Barlow?' Sage asked, thinking of the stunted little town they had just passed.

Kiebler laughed unpleasantly. 'Barlow's not a town where men pay for what they want. If they did, they'd relieve you of your poke before you had left town.'

Sage nodded. 'Tough town, is it?'

'Tough, dirty, heartless and cruel.' Kiebler was scowling now. It was an unusual expression on the cheerful sutler's face.

'You've done business with the town before?'

'I tried to once before the army came in and I got my sutler's commission. I had a break-in twice a week, all sorts of pilfering and some downright malicious damage.'

Sage now was thoughtful as the team followed a more clearly defined road toward Mackay's farm.

It was a little odd to Sage's way of thinking. Most frontier towns were very needful of some sort of store, so much so that they would never risk driving them off any more than they would the local doctor.

'What do they do now for the needfuls?'

'If it doesn't come in a bottle, they don't seem to have any use for it.'

Sage nodded. 'Barlow sounds like a nasty town — I'll avoid it.' He added, 'The army post must've seemed like a fine, well-ordered place to work after that.'

'Yes, the army has its rules, and

anyway none of the troopers would stand for seeing me harassed — if I pulled out, that would leave them with nothing.'

Sage smiled his understanding, thinking that, also — although the soldiers didn't have much to spend on payday — they were a steady, predictable source of income.

'I see old Ben Mackay standing over there near that twin-pine,' Kiebler said, relighting his pipe. 'I'll tell him what I need and ask him where he wants us to start, though I already know. We'll be taking the cherry boxes first. The apples are in sacks, we can put them on top of them. There's only a little damage done to the produce if you're careful about what you're doing.'

Sage just nodded. No one was asking for his opinion. He was only hired help for the day. Which gave him cause to think as the wagon team was guided toward where Mackay stood watching — how was his horse doing on this morning? It was too much to hope that it could have been miraculously cured overnight, but Sage had little time to waste. The storm had broken, the sun was beaming down pleasantly, and the long vengeance trail to Trinity was beckoning insistently again.

Charles Mackay was a little bulldog of a man: small nose, small ears, grayish complexion, sagging jowls and a tuft of red hair which showed when he removed his hat to wipe his scalp. He had small, uncertain eyes which seemed to brighten a little as he stepped forward to welcome Kiebler.

'Brought some help, did you?' Mackay said as the two men shook hands.

'Ah, the work's getting too hard for my failing back, Charles. I needed some young muscle along.'

Mackay's eyes lifted to study and evaluate Sage Paxton. 'Don't look like a soldier to me.'

'No,' Kiebler laughed, 'he's not. The captain would never loan me a trooper for something like this. The way he sees it army business and my business are two different and separate jobs. This is Sage Paxton, he was temporarily displaced by the storm.'

'And wasn't it coming down!' Charles Mackay said, seeming to have forgotten all about Sage. He hadn't. 'Paxton, you say. It seems I've heard that name before.'

'It's a new one to me,' Kiebler said, although he had said the same thing to Sage the night before. He was not the Paxton they had heard of; that one lived in Trinity. Sage sat the wagon seat, looking around innocently. He heard Mackay speak again. 'Tall, dark and handsome, isn't he?'

'Well,' Kiebler said without hesitation, 'he's tall enough and you can see that dark hair of his; as far as being handsome, I'd have to let a woman make a judgement on that.'

'Just make sure it ain't no woman around here,' Mackay said. He added, 'Cherry boxes are in the barn, usual number. We can tally them if you like.'

'I trust you, Charles, like I hope you trust me.'

'I trust you fine, Kiebler — if I didn't, we wouldn't be doing business together.'

With that Charles Mackay turned on his heel and stumped back toward his house. Kiebler started the team and wagon again.

'What was that about?' Sage asked.

'What? Oh, the part about you being handsome? Charles Mackay has a pretty young daughter, and he worries about her — his wife ran off with a traveling man. Don't let him trouble you, Sage. Mackay is no one to worry about.'

The wagon was pulled into the barn and Sage got down to eye the carefully stacked boxes of cherries. 'You want to count these?' he asked Kiebler, who had removed his coat prior to the work.

'No, you heard what I told Mackay. His word is good enough for me. A man wouldn't get far if he kept shorting his buyer, would he?'

'How do you want to do this?'

'I'll climb up on the wagon bed and stack the boxes if you don't mind handing them up. I've had some experience on the best way to load.'

'Whatever you say — I'm just the labor.'

Sage began picking up the cherry flats, two at a time, and carrying them to the rear of the wagon. He was ahead of Kiebler in the loading, so he simply stacked the boxes on the wagon's tailgate. It took no more than an hour. It was light work, cool in the barn, but even so Kiebler was perspiring when he clambered down from the wagon bed.

'I am getting old!' Kiebler said, mopping at his expansive brow with his handkerchief. 'I'm glad I brought you along, Sage.'

'I'm glad I came. What would I have done with myself back at the fort but sit and worry and get mad at myself for getting myself in this fix.'

'Now for the apples,' Kiebler said after a few minutes' rest.

These were in burlap bags at the other end of the barn, and harder to load only because they had to be carried one at a time over the shoulder. On a tag sewn to the tie at the top of the bags it said 'Apples, fifty pounds', but some of these sure seemed heavier to Sage. He could see why Kiebler had asked him to come along. The store-keeper would have had quite a time of it loading the sacks by himself.

With the last sack delivered to the tailgate, Sage removed his hat, scratched at his head and waited while Kiebler arranged things to his liking. 'What now?' Sage asked.

'Get the tarp out of that side box and throw it over and tie it down,' Kiebler answered. He was sitting on the tailgate now, breathing rather heavily. 'I'll go over and talk to Mackay, pay him off.'

Sage did as he was asked, removing the heavy canvas tarpaulin from its storage box and spreading it over the produce. That was not as simple as it sounded, and before he had finished

Kiebler had returned from the house accompanied by Charles Mackay.

'Ready?' Kiebler called out.

'Soon as I finish lashing down the back.' Sage started toward the rear of the wagon.

'Never figured out why you bother with a tarp,' Mackay was saying.

'If something comes loose on the grade, I don't want to go chasing rolling apples down the hillside.'

Mackay laughed and they started talking about something else. Sage didn't try to hear them. His attention had been caught by something else. Tying his final knots in the ropes he caught a glimpse of an unexpected sight. Two small boots projected from under the tarp, showing at the very edge of the wagon bed. Peeling the tarp back a little Sage saw wide dark eyes looking back at him fearfully. The girl's lips moved, but she formed no words, simply shook her head with those pleading eyes fixed on his.

They had a stowaway on board.

The young woman — it had to be Mackay's daughter, did it not? — had slipped into the wagon while Sage's attention was elsewhere. Sage did not wish to be involved in anyone else's trouble, neither did he think it was his place to thwart the girl's plan for escape — if that was what it was.

It would have caused much more of an uproar if he called out to Mackay than to simply pretend he had noticed nothing. Finishing his knots, he walked back to where Kiebler already was sitting on the wagon seat.

'All done?' he asked as Sage climbed aboard.

'We're ready.'

Kiebler lifted a hand to Mackay, who stepped aside as the wagon was drawn out of the barn and into the bright, clear light of day.

They rode silently along the trail through the forest, hearing only the chatter of the squirrels and the squawking of blue jays. Sage thought he heard a small scrabbling sound coming

32

from the back of the wagon, but Kiebler had not heard it and he decided to say nothing about it.

The dark rider appeared ahead of them as they crested the hill and again started down toward Fort Vasquez.

'Who's that?' Sage asked as the menacing, lone rider approached them. Kiebler's eyes flickered that way, narrowed against the glare of sunlight.

'It looks like Austin Szabo,' the sutler said. 'Sage — remember what I said about Charles Mackay? That he was not a man to worry about? Austin Szabo is a different sort of man. Don't give him any reason to look twice at us.'

'Why would I? What would he want with us, anyway?'

'Sometimes Szabo doesn't need a reason; he just feels like shooting.'

'Who is he, anyway?' Sage asked as the lone rider drew nearer. 'The law in Barlow or something?'

'Barlow has never had any law and never will have. Austin Szabo is what you might call the town boss there. And he's plenty tough. Remember, I told you that I once tried to start a store in that town. I've met Szabo and I know who and what he is. If he looks at you, look away.'

Sage nodded though he kept his eyes on the rider. He did not believe in ignoring trouble or hiding from it. The man — Szabo — he saw now was riding a dark-brown horse, nearly black, carried two Winchester rifles in scabbards and had two belted pistols. The man either liked guns a lot or had much use for them.

'Can't see any reason why he'd be interested in us,' Sage said.

'I don't think he is,' Kiebler answered in a lowered voice. 'From what Mackay told me in his house, it's his daughter, Gwen, that Szabo is interested in. And he seems ready to buy, bargain or bully Mackay into letting him have her.'

'A nice fellow,' Sage said, turning his eyes down now. He thought of the girl he had seen under the tarp of the wagon. If that had been Gwen Mackay, and it seemed it must be, she had good reason for wanting to escape the farm. He was all the more glad that he had not given her away.

'No, he isn't,' Kiebler said, finally replying. 'He is not a nice man. He is the exact opposite of nice, whatever that is.'

The rider was abreast of them now. A strong-looking man with sturdy features and no expression at all in his eyes. He focused his adder eyes on Sage and then looked down at Kiebler, who nodded his head slightly in recognition. No words were exchanged. Szabo continued along the trail. Sage saw the man slow his horse and seem to look back at the wagon, but he did not return.

It was none of his business. Szabo, Gwen Mackay, the town of Barlow had nothing to do with Sage Paxton, and he was glad of it. It was enough, however, to make returning to the trail to Trinity seem that much more urgent. He had his own mission to resume and it had nothing to do with the spats, loves, hates and desires of these hill folks.

It had to do only with killing a man.

3

The fort stood upon the junction of the two rain-swollen rivers, looking stolid, purposeful but somehow futile against the background of sprawling primitive land surrounding it. The main gate stood open and Kiebler rolled his wagon through with a wave of the hand to the men standing guard.

The sutler nodded toward the front door of his shop where four or five soldiers crowded the plank walk. One of them shouted out to Kiebler, who waved again before guiding his team between two buildings to draw up in a loading area behind his store.

'If I could afford a clerk, I'd hire one,' Kiebler said, halting the horses and setting the brake. 'Those boys out front are eager to throw their money away this morning.' Kiebler drew in his lower lip thoughtfully. 'It's close to payday; it must be tobacco they're so impatient for.'

Sage couldn't follow that logic if he was meant to. Grunting a response he stepped down from the wagon and stretched. 'What do you want me to do?' he called up.

'Just get the tarp off and stowed. I'll show you in a few minutes where I want the produce stored,' Kiebler said, climbing down himself. 'First I've got some anxious troopers to see to.'

'Right,' was Sage's short reply. He began untying the ropes which held the tarp as Kiebler entered the store via a back door. Untie the ropes, stow the tarp in the wagon's side box . . . and then what?

That is, there was a stowaway to be dealt with. Now they had smuggled her on to an army post. What was to be done with her? If she was still there . . .

Pulling the tarpaulin aside, Sage saw the same small girl, the same confused, frightened eyes looking up at him like some small wild beast he had captured and which wished to bolt but had no idea of where to go.

'End of the line, Gwen,' Sage told her. 'You'll have to hop down now.'

'They'll find me!'

'That seems likely. You didn't think your plan through very well, did you?' Sage set to work spreading the canvas tarp out on the ground so that it could be neatly folded. Gwen had hopped down, staggering as she hit the ground. Probably her legs had fallen asleep on her.

'Where should I go?' she asked Sage. She had taken one corner of the tarp to help him double it. Her eyes flickered around anxiously: a small rabbit caught in a snare.

'I couldn't tell you that,' Sage said, lifting his eyes. 'Maybe you should go to the camp commander, ask him for help.'

'Captain Rowland?' She laughed disparagingly. 'All he'd do is tell me to go home, maybe assign a couple of troopers to escort me and curse me for having cost him two men for the day.'

'You knew where the wagon was headed. Surely you must have considered these things before.'

They folded the tarp the other way. 'I knew, but Mr Kiebler, I know, is a kindly man. I thought he might have some ideas. Then I saw you and there was a kind look about you as well. I thought — I hoped — that between the two of you men you could come up with a plan to help me out of my mess.'

They folded again, transforming the bulky tarp into a neat rectangle which would fit in the side box of the wagon. As they worked, Sage watched the small woman. Her eyes were still deeply concerned, her face fearful. She exhaled tiny puffs of breath as she worked, apparently taking the small task seriously. She was a pretty little bob of a girl, well assembled and Sage could see why Austin Szabo was willing to go to extremes to have her.

And do what? Return with her to that stink hole of an outlaw town, Barlow?

That must have been a part of the reason behind Gwen Mackay's fear. To be captured by a black knight of an outlaw and taken to his slovenly castle . . . one of many fears the girl probably carried.

Snapping himself back from conjecture, Sage told her as they packed the heavy tarp away, 'Maybe Kiebler does have some sort of idea. Maybe he knows some frontier woman who would take you in.'

'And you?' She had those wide dark eyes fixed on Sage as he closed and latched the side box.

'Me?' He hesitated and tried to produce a laugh, at which he failed. Leaning against the wagon Sage crossed his arms and said, 'I've got someplace to go, and I'm going to be riding hard and long to get there. There'll be trouble at the end of the trail. Besides, I don't know a soul in Trinity, not a decent person, anyway.'

'Trinity . . . ?' Gwen's eyes seemed to glaze over a little; then they brightened.

'I know people in Trinity — at least I think I do. My mother's sisters — two maiden aunts of mine — have a little house there.'

'Good luck. It's a long walk to Trinity,' Sage said in a manner which was not kindly. He turned toward the back door of the store, felt Gwen's insistent fingers on his shirt sleeve and turned to look down at her eyes, now hopeful.

'You must have a horse,' she said.

'I do. I have one crippled-up horse and one rider for him — me.'

'Maybe I can find another one,' Gwen said with unfounded optimism.

'Not on an army post,' Sage answered. 'And the ones they do have wear a US brand and are meant to be kept.'

'But maybe Kiebler knows where I can come by one — or the troopers. Those boys ride far and wide. There must be some small farms around here, some with a horse to spare.'

'You have money with you, then.'

'No,' Gwen said with a slight stutter.

'That seems to put another kink in your plan, doesn't it? You'd have to know of a place where you could purchase a horse, walk to it, convince someone to let you have it for no money and avoid Austin Szabo the whole time.' Sage didn't mean for that to sound cruel, but apparently it did. Gwen's eyes clouded up and he thought she was about to cry.

'Szabo,' she said in a low voice as she studied the ground beneath her feet. 'That's right; he will find me.'

'That's why I advised you to walk over to the commanding officer's office and ask for help. Not even Szabo would be reckless enough to try to snatch you from the army.'

'Wouldn't he?' Gwen said. 'You don't know Austin Szabo very well, do you?'

'No,' Sage said without reflection, 'and I don't wish to or intend to.'

'You'd just give me over to him!'

'You're not mine to give over, Gwen. I don't know you either, and I have nothing to do with your situation. I'm only a long-riding, lone man who happens to have got stuck here for a few days.'

'You have something important to do?' she asked, and now Sage found that she was annoying him with her persistence.

'Yes, I do. It's very important: I have to kill a man.'

'Oh!' she gasped as she stepped away from him, her fingers dropping from his sleeves. 'You're just one of them, then.'

'I'm not one of anybody. You asked me a question about something that's none of your business and I answered you,' Sage said. The girl was getting to be a nuisance and he had no interest in continuing the conversation with her. If it weren't for those very sad dark eyes . . .

How can a man feel shame about something that's none of his doing and that he can do nothing to remedy? He could, Sage thought, if he was a fool.

44

He put his hand on the doorknob and said gruffly, 'Wait a minute and you can talk to Kiebler. I'll see if his soldier customers have all gone.'

'Mr Kiebler will have an idea,' Gwen said. 'He's a kind man,' she added, as if it were an admonition.

'Yes, he is,' Sage answered, though he doubted that Kiebler with the best of intentions could figure a way to get a runaway girl pursued by an obsessed thug safely away from a military post without so much as a dollar or a pony to ride.

The sutler's shop seemed empty and silent with only a single ring of the cash register's bell to indicate that anyone at all was there.

'Oh, Paxton,' Kiebler said, looking up from his till. 'You startled me a little.'

'I've brought something to startle you more. You still haven't shown me where to store the produce.'

'Back in the rear pantry,' Kiebler said, his brow furrowing a little with concern, 'but what do you mean about bringing something that will startle me?'

'He means me,' Gwen Mackay said, stepping into the store through the back door.

Kiebler halted his movements. His mouth didn't exactly drop open, but seemed incapable of forming words. Certainly his eyes widened behind his spectacles. The man was speechless. Sage broke through the silence. 'You mean that room with the heavy door on the left down the hallway?'

'Yes, yes,' Kiebler said in a shaky voice. 'Near the potatoes.' He was babbling now, and Sage returned to the wagon without hearing the rest of his rapid, scrambled conversation with Gwen Mackay.

When Sage returned, a sack of apples over his shoulder, the two were still talking, leaning across the counter of the store. Gwen's voice was low, pleading; Kiebler's face was drawn with concern. He was shaking his head heavily. Sage dropped his sack where indicated and returned to the wagon. The two were still talking, Gwen's voice entreating.

Sage, himself, saw the problem as unsolvable, and he did not strain to catch their words. He was not a man without compassion, but neither could he offer a solution — besides he had his own problems, his own trail to ride.

During his tenth load, he saw that Gwen had retreated to a corner chair to sob and feel sorry for herself. Kiebler halted Sage and asked sharply, 'Well, young man, what do you propose to do to solve this?'

'Me?' Sage said blankly. He had considered himself relieved of the situation once Gwen Mackay had Kiebler's ear. 'What have I to do with this?'

'Certainly more than I do,' the old man replied. 'After all, you're the one who brought her here.'

'I did not,' Sage said. 'You were driving the wagon.'

'Yes, but I didn't know that she was

on it. According to the girl, you did.'

'I didn't turn her in, that's all. Would you have done otherwise?'

'Charles Mackay is a . . . well, maybe not a friend of mine, but a business associate.'

'Then you would have turned her in, even knowing Austin Szabo as you do?' Both men glanced at the forlorn little woman in the corner chair, her eyes now lifted toward them. 'No,' Kiebler admitted heavily. 'I don't think I would have done that, Paxton — now what do we do?'

'I could only think to tell her to go to Captain Rowland and explain.'

'You don't know Rowland, he'd only order her to leave his camp. And he'd give me hell for allowing this to happen. Then he'd start wondering about you and your horse. Rowland is not a bad officer, he just doesn't like civilians interfering in the orderly operations of his fort. He could ruin me if he really got riled — throw me off the post.'

'Then you'll have to get her off

before he learns anything of it,' Sage said.

'*I*, I alone? Then you're just shrugging off your responsibility?'

'I never had any responsibility in this,' Sage said with just a little heat.

'And I never had any responsibility in taking you in out of the rain and finding a stable for your horse,' Kiebler said, his eyes now growing shrewd. Sage sighed heavily. He got the point. 'Now, then, how do we get her off the post and get her somewhere else, Paxton?'

'We get her off the same way we got her on,' Sage believed. 'As to where she might go, I haven't an idea in the world. Don't you? It's your territory around here.'

'Maybe,' Kiebler said, mopping at his broad forehead with his handkerchief again. 'I need to think a little longer about that. Finish bringing in the produce and I'll try to come up with something.'

The apples stored, the cherries in their place, Sage stopped for a breather, seating himself on the back porch of the store. The sky was high, clear but for a few straggling clouds, and the air was as fresh as it can only be after the passing of a storm. From somewhere nearby he could hear the sounds of a blacksmith at his anvil and farther away the shouted commands of a drill sergeant. He could not hear voices inside the store. Maybe Kiebler had decided to keep the business closed until this matter with Gwen was solved.

How, Sage wondered, was his gray horse? Well enough to travel if care were taken to stick to even ground and ride easily? Every hour he delayed was an hour given to his adversary to make his escape. Stagecoaches ran through Trinity; his man could step aboard one and vanish in no time, extending Sage's search for days, weeks, years — for surely he would pursue his prey no matter how long it took. Trinity was the place to catch him, now before his man was alerted and could flee.

Rising, abandoning his circular thoughts,

Sage went into the store. Gwen was alone, still sitting in the corner of the room, hands knotted together. A small, pitiful creature, the sight of her tugged at Sage's heart just a little. A woman expecting no help, waiting for her brutal suitor to track her down.

'Where's Kiebler?' he snapped. Gwen winced as if he had slapped her.

'He went out,' she answered, expressing the obvious.

'To see Captain Rowland?'

'We saw Captain Rowland ride out with a patrol not a few minutes ago.'

Then where? As if in answer to his unspoken question, Sage heard a horse, walking slowly, approach the store. Peering out the curtain, Sage saw Kiebler leading his saddled gray toward the store. The horse was not limping noticeably, but it moved gingerly, its right haunch still obviously bothering it. That was one problem solved — Sage had had no idea how he was to cross the yard, retrieve his horse if fit for travel at all and return without the first sergeant, Rowland or someone else noticing and questioning his presence on the post.

'He's walking it around back,' Sage said to Gwen, who gave no response, just sat there silently in her misery.

Walking toward the rear of the store, Sage could hear the slow heavy clopping of his horse's hoofs and saw Kiebler appear around the corner of the building, leading the gray.

The little man looked serious and anxious as he had the right to be. He drew the gray up at the rear hitching post, tying it loosely. Sage's first thoughts were on his horse and he walked to the animal, stroking its muzzle before going to its hind leg to feel the tendon there.

Kiebler spoke with unexpected force. 'Turn the wagon around and break out the tarp again.'

'We're leaving?'

'We are,' Kiebler said.

'Going . . . ?'

'Turn the wagon around and break

out the tarp again,' Kiebler repeated, breaking out a tone of command which seemed totally foreign to the mild store-keeper's usual manner. Sage turned away from his own horse.

'What did you tell Rowland?'

'The captain rode out with a small party of troopers. I told the first sergeant that Mackay had made a mistake in his count and that I was going to have to go back up to his farm.'

'My horse — ' Sage began, but this was not the day for Kiebler's patience to endure.

'Do what I told you, Paxton! You must see that we have to get the girl off the post before the captain returns.'

Sage only nodded and set to his tasks. With the wagon turned and the tarp spread out over the bed, Kiebler glanced once from the back door and then, taking Gwen's elbow, hurried her toward the wagon. The girl slid up on to the rough wagon bed and was hastily covered with the tarp. Sage wondered if the troopers at the gate might challenge him, but then remembered that they had seen him already once this morning and had not bothered to ask who he was or what he was doing there. So leaving the wagon and its living contraband to Kiebler, Sage hesitantly mounted his gray horse and walked it slowly toward the gate.

They were passed without incident although Sage seemed to feel the eyes of the sentries probing him, seeking to penetrate the secret hidden beneath the canvas tarpaulin. No one spoke. Kiebler raised a hand in greeting as always; the wagon went on without any cries of alarm being shouted. Then they were out on the open land again, and after two turns of the road they found themselves on the lower ground near the river where no eyes from the fort could see them. They were free.

Free? An odd word for it. Free to do what?

Kiebler had halted the wagon to allow Gwen to slip from under the tarp and on to the bench seat beside him. Sage walked his ill-used gray horse up beside them and asked both of them, 'Well, have we any idea of where we're headed yet?'

'What does it matter to you?' Kiebler grumbled. 'You've got your horse back.'

'I can't say why it matters,' Sage said honestly, 'but it does.'

Gwen was sitting, hands folded, watching Sage curiously with an expression he could not read. He turned his own gaze away to watch the Vasquez River, still frothing and running from bank to bank with the run-off from the storm, as it rushed southward. Above the mountains, he noticed there was a legion of newly arrived storm clouds. Running into another storm would not do — he could not risk being again stranded on the plains. He had to make Trinity or at least reach some settlement he could hole up in.

The wind at their backs lifted the fine hair from Kiebler's scalp as he wiped off his brow prior to replanting his hat again.

'I'm thinking we could give Mike Currant's place a try,' the sutler said, glancing at Gwen and then again at Sage. 'There's not much of Mike to brag about, but his old woman, Ellie, is the salt of the earth.'

Kiebler had obviously not discussed this with Gwen, who now sat wooden-faced, as enduring as an orphaned Indian. What could the girl say? She had to be somewhere; it seemed as if where no longer mattered to her.

'I don't know this Mike Currant,' Sage said, 'don't know where his place is, but if we're going to go there, we'd better start moving. It looks fearfully like it's going to storm again overnight.'

Kiebler nodded, slapped the reins against his horses' flanks and the wagon began creaking forward, Gwen looking vacantly ahead. Sage shook off that occasional guilt feeling he was carrying and rode on again, keeping the still-injured gray to the slow speed of

Kiebler's team, though the gray seemed to wish to move on at a quicker pace, perhaps not realizing the seriousness of its injury.

They traveled on an easy two more miles, no one speaking, until, at a place where the river slowed and flattened due to the land opening up, they saw a small house standing in a gray mirror of storm runoff in the low valley ahead.

'They just about got themselves flooded out, didn't they,' Kiebler said, apparently to himself.

'It was more rain than anybody could have expected,' Sage said. He might have been speaking to himself as well. No one answered.

There were four scraggly willow trees in front of the house, all tilted away from the prevailing north wind. Nearing the house, they saw a scowling man with a beard, a heavy straw broom in his hands, sweeping the storm's residue from the front porch. Gwen stiffened, seeming not to like the looks of the man at first glance, and if first appearances were anything to go by, Sage didn't either.

Slovenly, in oversized twill pants and red suspenders wearing a blue shirt which showed stains across the front as if he had spat tobacco juice on himself, his hair was lank and greasy. He didn't look as if he'd shaved for at least a week: salt and pepper whiskers decorated his slack jowls.

Tilting his broom against the wall of the house, he stepped off the porch and came forward to meet Kiebler's halted wagon, thumbs hooked into the waistband of his trousers.

'Nothin' to sell, nothing I want to buy,' he said to Kiebler, though his eyes were not on the sutler, but on Gwen.

'I wasn't here on business,' Kiebler said. 'Is Ellie around?'

'No, she isn't,' Currant said. 'She won't be comin' back.'

'Why's that?' Kiebler asked, looking toward the house.

'Because she's dead. She died dead all of the sudden and just left all of this housework to me, keeping me from my regular chores,' the man complained.

Glancing around the place, Sage couldn't see what work he was being kept from. No soil was turned for planting and there wasn't a sign of any sort of livestock that might need tending.

'What's that small package you got there, Kiebler?' Mike Currant asked, leaning nearer to study Gwen more personally.

'Just someone who needs a place to stay for a while. That's why I was asking about Ellie.'

'As I told you, Ellie's gone . . . but I could use a girl to cook and clean around the house for me,' Currant said. 'She could work for room and board.'

Sage saw Gwen quiver slightly as the leering man looked her over too closely. Sage answered before Kiebler could. 'No, thanks, that won't do. We're looking for a place with a woman to care for her.'

Currant's eyes shifted to Sage as if

noticing him for the first time. The gaze they held was not a pleasant one and Sage let his eyes drop, looking away from Currant's angry eyes toward the long-running river. This was no time for more trouble. The road to Trinity was beckoning and the man at the end of that trail still needed killing.

4

Mike Currant's little mouth formed a sort of twisted imitation of a smile. The man's eyes remained hard. It was obvious what Currant had in mind. Perhaps he had thought he could wheedle or bully Kiebler into doing as he wished. The tall man on the gray horse appeared to be a different proposition altogether. He didn't like the nearness of his hand to his pistol, nor his steady gaze. Currant gave it up.

'Find her another place then, and be damned!' he said before huffing off toward his house. Kiebler watched him go with a sort of disgusted resignation. Gwen's tensed body seemed to have relaxed a little.

'Where next?' Sage asked.

'Where *next*?' Kiebler asked, turning on the bench seat to glare at Sage Paxton. 'There is no next! There's no other place close by, and I've got to get back to my store. It's not like I'm some footloose cavalier who can run around the country looking for a place to put the girl.' His look seemed to place Sage in that category, one he was not prepared to shoulder.

'You said you'd try to do something for her,' Sage said.

'And so I have, Paxton. I have tried and failed — now it's up to you. You're the one who brought this down on us.'

It was a hell of a rough way to speak in front of the girl, and must have left her feeling smaller and more helpless than ever.

'You can't be thinking of just abandoning her,' Sage said, realizing that he himself sounded as if they were trying to drop an unwanted dog along the road.

'How can I . . . ? Look, Paxton, I've got work to attend to, and plenty of it. I gave it my best shot. It didn't work out, all right? If you think you can do better, be my guest. You've no place to go, nothing to do anyway.' Kiebler had begun to mop at his face with his handkerchief. The little man did have a kind heart; this was probably tearing at him.

'Where's the next village?' Sage asked sharply. 'In the direction of Trinity, I mean. I can't be doubling back.'

'There's a place called Drovers' Springs not more than twenty-five miles west,' Kiebler said. He glanced across his shoulder to the north. 'You should be able to make it before the new storm sets in.'

'On a lame horse,' Sage said, feeling distinctly put-upon.

'I'm sure you've ridden more than that much in a day,' Kiebler said with a touch of resigned anxiety.

'I'm sure I have but not with a lame horse carrying double and a pack of outlaws behind me.'

'What do you mean?' Kiebler asked, thumbing his spectacles up on his nose.

'What do you think I mean! Do you think that Austin Szabo is just going to give it up, shrug his shoulders and go back to Barlow town?'

'No,' Kiebler said, pausing before he spoke, 'I suppose he won't.'

Sage sat there in the twisting wind, his horse standing three-legged beneath him, and looked across the gray-white frothing river beyond which lay the trail to Trinity, once toward the farmhouse where the sullen Mike Currant had returned to his sweeping, and once at the girl with the unhappy, confused eyes, who had turned her head to look hopefully toward him.

'Oh, the hell with it all,' he muttered. 'Step down, Gwen, we've got a long way to travel.'

While Kiebler turned his team back toward Fort Vasquez, his face reflecting relief and shame at once, Sage Paxton started his gray horse into motion. With the girl riding behind him Sage allowed the horse no freedom to step out, but kept a tight rein on the injured animal. As a result their pace as they plodded toward the distant town of Drovers'

Springs was incredibly slow.

Sage kept the horse to the riverside trail, which now and then became hidden by the risen water of the river in flood. The girl's grip around his waist was light but secure. Sage scolded himself mentally for actually finding the thought of her against him comforting and oddly cheering. Not that there was any real cheer in Sage's heart just then — he was grim, a stalking wolf. He could not remember when he had last actually felt cheerful. He wanted to apologize to Gwen for the constant scowl he wore, the grouchiness of his manner, but he would not. He didn't need to draw her closer to him. They would not be long together, and things were suitable as they were.

The rush of the river was a constant presence on his right, gurgling, slapping, eddying, rushing or milling depending on the mood of Nature and the river channel's composition. The Vasquez was wider now, more placid, though he would not have wished to cross it even here.

The sky began to darken, shading his mood. The storm clouds were moving toward them far too quickly. Not again! He could not be caught out on the trail again on such a night as he had endured. He hurried the gray on a little more rapidly.

'How far is it to Drovers' Springs?' he asked, turning his head.

'I don't know. I've never been there. Didn't Mr Kiebler say that it was twenty-five miles away from Currant's place?'

'That's right, he did. I think that it was more of a guess than anything else.' Sage turned the horse slightly and ducked his head. They were moving through an area now rife with willow trees and spotty sycamores. There would be clearer riding farther away from the river, but he did not wish to lose his way. The river provided direction; the trees provided cover.

'How far do you think we've come?'

Gwen asked, her words muffled against his back.

'Not half that,' Sage said, and then added unkindly, 'I can't expect my horse to make any speed traveling like this.'

Her grip on him loosened, tightened and loosened again. Was she thinking that he wanted her to get down? He touched her hands where they joined around his waist in what he hoped was a reassuring gesture. He did not want her to dismount. He would leave no woman alone, afoot in the wild country, especially this one who might still be pursued by a dark-hearted gunman.

Why then had he bothered to say anything at all? Just putting sound to his own unhappiness, he decided. He would have apologized under normal circumstances, but a contrary part of him felt like he owed her no apology.

Glancing up, Sage saw that the sky was nearly roofed over now with dark, threatening clouds. He swallowed a curse. He could do nothing about it but continue, guiding his horse carefully, slowly — for now and then he could feel the gray drag its leg and hesitate as if it would like to pull up, which was probably the case.

Instead he kept it moving on. Was Kiebler's guess of twenty-five miles on the shy side or was it much farther? How often could the storekeeper have visited Drovers' Springs, if he ever had? It was likely that he had never actually been to the plains settlement. What would he have gone there for? Someone had once told Kiebler of the place, and that someone had probably been guessing at the distance himself.

Something tapped against Sage's hat and he thought at first that it was only a bit of dry detritus falling from the overhanging trees, but after that first tap a steady sound like gravel sifting downward began and, as the wind picked up and the clouds lowered, Sage knew that it had begun to rain again. The river's face became pocked with thousands of pits.

Gwen had only her waist-length leather jacket and her low-tugged black Stetson to keep the water off her, Sage little more. He still had his black slicker tied behind with his bedroll, but he was reluctant to stop and recover it — or offer it to Gwen. The rain was not as insistent as it had been the day before, not so heavy, the wind not gusting with such ferocity. It did shake the trees around them and rattle the brush along the river, but maybe, he thought, it would hold back for a little while, even lighten up some as they wove their way out of the weather's reach. Faint hope, but Sage clung to it as the gray, now clearly unhappy and stiffening, carried them along the riverside trail.

'Sage!' Gwen yelled out and he turned to look at her. Beyond Gwen he could see an onrushing horseman in a yellow rain slicker weaving his way through the woods. He was coming on with a purpose. Reflex alone caused Sage to heel the gray horse sharply. There was no choice, it was do or die, and the gray plunged ahead as rapidly as it could, dividing willow brush, veering around trees.

The clouds were low, wind-tormented. The rain cut his visibility to almost nothing. Appearing suddenly like a black bar across the trail a low-hanging sycamore bough manifested itself. Sage half-turned, hooked his arm around Gwen and ducked under the bough, tugging the girl down with him.

That was close, it was very close. Had he been riding any faster he would never have . . . the man behind them was riding faster, much faster, leaving him less time to react. Pounding up the trail in pursuit, he came to the same bough, and there was nothing he could do to avoid it.

There was a muffled but distinct cracking sound above the storm's constant dirge, and Sage saw the man fall to the earth. He already knew the man would not be getting up again. The crack had proven that his neck was no match for ten inches of sycamore wood struck at speed. Sage turned his laboring gray and rode back that way, halting within a few yards of the man in the yellow slicker. His head was turned around unnaturally, his dead eyes looking nearly across his back at Sage Paxton. Nearby a confused bay horse circled and then halted.

Sage slipped to the ground, Gwen behind him as they approached the man through the falling rain. 'Who is it?' she asked in a taut whisper. 'Do we know him? Is it Austin Szabo?'

'No,' Sage said, crouching down over the body. 'It's Mike Currant.'

'Currant! But why would he bother to come trailing us this far? What did he want of us?'

'He wanted to see if you wore a petticoat under your jeans.'

'What does that mean? You make no sense, Sage,' Gwen said dully.

'No, I don't. Forget it; I don't know what I meant either.' He rose, looking around through the screen of the gray rain. He expected no one else; there should be no one else. But then he hadn't expected Mike Currant either.

'Do we have to bury him?' Gwen asked through chattering teeth. The wind was buffeting them more roughly now.

'No, I won't waste the time on him. We have to keep moving,' he said, looking skyward.

'Well, it will be easier now,' Gwen told him. He looked at her with a question in his eyes. 'We've got two horses now, haven't we?' she said, gesturing toward the bay Mike Currant had been riding.

Sage nodded glumly; he supposed that was *something*. 'The gray will appreciate it,' he said, stroking the horse's damp muzzle as it nudged him.

'Do you want to ride the bay?' Gwen asked, her eyes bright and almost eager. Sage shook his head.

'No, I'll stick with the gray. I know his ways.'

'All right.' She gathered up the wet

reins to the standing bay and said, 'I don't suppose we have to ride together now, if you aren't of a mind to.'

'Yes, we do,' Sage said, whisking the water from his saddle. He reached for his tied-down slicker.

'Why?' she asked with what was nearly a smile. Sage nodded toward the crumpled figure of Mike Currant.

'We still don't know where Austin Szabo is. If a farmer like Currant could follow us, it's a pretty sure bet that a wild-country man like Szabo can.'

'He'd never find out,' Gwen objected. 'He doesn't know we started from the fort.'

'How many other places are there you could have gone? And how many other ways than in Kiebler's wagon? He'll remember passing the wagon on the trail.'

'And follow this morning's wagon tracks? The rain has probably washed them away.'

'Maybe, but it hasn't washed Kiebler's memory free.'

73

'Szabo wouldn't hurt the old man!'

'Wouldn't he? You told me yourself that Szabo had no fear of the soldiers there, and Captain Rowland is away now. Szabo is a murderous man, and Kiebler won't be able to protect himself well with saltwater taffy.'

Gwen shivered again, and Sage couldn't guess if it was the driving cold rain or the thought of meeting Austin Szabo in the open land which had caused it. He tossed her his slicker. 'Slip into this — it'll help some.'

She made her way into the black slicker, rolling up the sleeves, cinching it around her as tightly as possible, but it was still outrageously large on her. She looked like she was wearing a black tent.

Sage didn't spare a smile. 'Onward,' he said.

Side by side they plodded on, their horses equally tired. Currant's bay had been ridden hard and long. It was difficult to hold any sort of conversation above the constant storm.

Sage was soaked to the bone. He could get no wetter. He wished he had taken Mike Currant's rain slicker from the body, but he could not have. It was too much like looting the dead. It was nearly dark now, and it was not all because of the low, smothering clouds: it was getting close to sundown. They were going to have to cross the river, like it or not. They could not afford to miss Drovers' Springs. There was no other place to survive the night that either of them knew of for a hundred miles. If they missed that small outpost, they were going to die.

At each wide spot in the river, where the water flowed more shallowly and it seemed that the current was slower, Sage paused to peer out across the Vasquez. There was no telling where concealed sinks awaited the unwary traveler, where the current looking placid at one moment might rage and swell the next.

'We're going to have to risk it at some

point,' he muttered to Gwen through the rain.

'Can't we just take the ferry?' Gwen Mackay asked, lifting a pointing finger.

Frowning, his forehead furrowed, Sage looked toward the south where a light flickered in the dusky gloom. A ferry boat, drawn by lines which were towed by mules, was making its slow, current-buffeted way across the face of the turbulent Vasquez River not half a mile from where they sat.

Gwen, bless her, did not smile and Sage answered lightly, 'We'll give that a try first.'

He had been thinking of plunging the injured gray into the raging water, trying to cross under terrible conditions and now they were in sight of a ferry boat! That meant two things — safe passage and progress toward finding Drovers' Springs, for certainly no one had constructed a ferry crossing out in this wilderness on a whim. It was built to serve the needs of the townspeople nearby.

'Good thing you saw that,' Sage said. Gwen nodded.

'Good thing I did, because I don't know if I would have even attempted crossing the river on horseback.'

'Well, here it is and here we are — let's get over there and see where it's going to take us next.'

That was a large question for Gwen. As far as Sage was concerned there was only one way to travel on from here, and that was down the lonesome trail to Trinity to its eventual bloody end.

5

The town of Drovers' Springs, when they reached it after a fairly hazardous crossing on the river ferry, was about what Sage had expected. He had been to finer-looking towns, visited worse. The streets, what few of them there were, were awash with red mud. The gray fronts of the buildings fronting the main street looked melancholy, seeming to droop under the burden of the rain.

Sage had his traveling money still — enough to provide for one man riding what might be a one-way trail to Trinity. He had not accounted for a traveling companion. The horses were taken care of first. The gray horse's limp had grown more pronounced again. With the horses in the care of a good stable, they slogged across the muddy road and up one block to the local hotel. On its front window

'Drover's Rest' was painted in ornate red and gilt lettering. Gwen hesitated at the doorway.

'What's the matter?' Sage asked the little girl in the outsized black rain slicker.

'I haven't got any money,' Gwen answered, looking down.

'I know that,' Sage answered, 'I can lend you enough for a room.'

'I couldn't take money from a man,' Gwen said in a pathetic little voice. Rain was streaming from the hotel's awning, the cold wind was still gusting. Sage was wet clean through, and chilled. His mood was getting no better.

'Follow me in or stay out here for the night — it makes no difference to me.'

He opened the door and tramped into the warm white interior of the hotel. He heard a smaller pair of boots clicking along behind him as he crossed the floor toward the desk. The man behind the desk had a shiny head and wore gold-rimmed spectacles. He had already gestured for a boy to mop their tracks from the oak floor.

'Double room, sir?' the desk clerk asked.

'Two singles. Do you have baths here?'

'They can be brought and delivered in less than an hour.'

'Fine,' Sage said, as two keys were slid across the counter toward him. 'Have' — he glanced at the unhappy figure of Gwen Mackay — 'a bath sent to each room.'

Their upstairs rooms were opposite. Gwen tried to thank him, but Sage only nodded and entered his room. Stripping down as soon as he entered, he wrapped himself in a spare blanket which was folded at the foot of the bed. There was still a deep chill on him; he had hopes that a hot bath would return him to something near human comfort. A tapping at the door summoned Sage and he swung the door open to find a hotel employee, a kid of sixteen or so.

'Thought maybe you had brought my bath,' Sage said.

'That will take a while, sir. Do you require anything else?'

'Coffee and a small whiskey. And' — he glanced toward the sodden pile of clothes he had left on the floor — 'can anything be done to dry those out?'

'If you're not in a hurry I can have them hung up to dry in the kitchen, and ironed by morning.'

'No hurry, I don't need them to go to bed in. I thank you, son,' Sage said, slipping the boy a small tip. The kid took the tip expressionlessly, nodded and scooped up the bundle of Sage's rain-heavy garments.

A different worker delivered a quart pot of hot coffee within ten minutes along with a glass containing two fingers of good Kentucky bourbon. Sage tipped this boy too with a coin drawn from his dwindling purse. This was high living for him, but, he pondered, he might not have any further use for money soon.

He didn't allow himself to dwell on that. After drying his hair with a rough towel he drew his blanket still more tightly around him and seated himself in a corner rocker, sipping coffee and occasionally whiskey while waiting for his bathtub and hot water to be delivered, feeling for the moment like a king snug in his own tiny kingdom.

He listened to the constantly falling rain. Outside of that there were no other sounds audible across town. Everyone with any sense was inside out of the storm. The rain had muted the world. He had no concern about anyone — Austin Szabo, for example — following them into Drovers' Springs. Not on this night, under these conditions. Sage even managed to doze for a few minutes before his tub and the following procession of men carrying hot water to fill it with arrived. When this group was gone Sage lowered himself into the copper tub and its exquisite warmth, settled in with his whiskey glass in hand and dozed off once again.

Life was good.

After soaping down and rinsing he felt almost like a complete man. He rubbed his jaw, considered shaving and then decided that could wait until morning. He slipped in between the sheets of the bed and pulled the blankets tight around him. After a few minutes he no longer heard the insistent drumming of the rain against the hotel's roof. He was away from Drovers' Springs, away from the troubles of the world in some distant place where all was warmth and comfort.

Morning was a bright splash of gold against the window of Sage's hotel room. It was a harsh sort of awakening after the gloom and gray of recent days, but he knew he had to rise, and soon. There was a long trail awaiting him still. But, yawning, he rolled over in bed and covered himself tightly again. After the deprivation he had suffered lately, he was reluctant to leave his small paradise and step out of bed into the chill of the morning.

When he finally did spur himself into rising, he was surprised and slightly angered to realize that he was doing so not for the sake of his quest, but because of another human being for whose welfare he had tacitly assumed responsibility. That is, he was concerned about Gwen.

Why he should waste any more time concerning himself with the small, dark-haired woman was beyond him. She had simply popped into his life seeking his protection. He owed her nothing more. He had done all that could be expected of him, taking Gwen across the river in the night, finding a bed for her to tuck into. She was not a child; she had made her choices: let her live with them and solve her own problems.

Her condition was not a happy one, alone away from home, an angry and quite dangerous suitor probably on her trail. Without money, with no place to stay, it was an unenviable position, but, as Sage reminded himself again, the girl had made her choices.

There was a moment's confusion when Sage finally swung his legs to the floor, looked around and realized that he had no clothes to wear. He remembered now sending them out to be dried in the hotel kitchen. An expensive but probably necessary action. He could imagine trying to get into a cold, rain-heavy pair of jeans on this morning and being subsequently condemned to wearing them all day.

There was a thimbleful of whiskey in his glass from the night before, and nearly a cup of cold coffee in the pot. With his blanket still worn Indian-style he settled into the rocking chair once again and drank both.

He became growingly annoyed with himself. It was time to get moving. There was now no barrier between him and the end of his trail. He decided to look out into the hallway to search for a hotel employee who might have his clothes sent up. Almost at the same moment there was the light rapping of knuckles against the door to his room. Good. The hotel must have anticipated his need.

Walking that way, he swung the door open to find Gwen Mackay standing in the hall holding his clothes up on a wooden hanger. Silently he groaned; aloud he said, 'Good morning, what are you doing here?'

'I brought your clothes,' she said, holding them up. 'I saw them hanging on your doorknob and figured you would be needing them.'

Holding the clothes high so that they did not touch the floor, Gwen entered, her eyes averted, but not deliberately so from the tall, whiskered man wrapped in a striped blanket.

'Fine,' Sage said, 'thank you.'

'Do you want me to leave?' Gwen asked. 'While you dress, I mean.'

'It doesn't matter to me,' Sage said. 'You might want to spend a few minutes looking out the window, though.'

He noticed that her own jeans and

flannel shirt were dry, that she had managed to do something with her hair, pinning it up. He felt a little awkward and primitive suddenly.

With Gwen staring out the window at the ramshackle town of Drovers' Springs, he stepped into his dry, creased jeans and stamped into his boots, finding them still damp. Shrugging into his shirt but not buttoning it, he retrieved soap and razor from his saddle-bags. What the point in shaving was at this point he could not have said, but he applied a half-dozen strops to the razor from the leather hung on the wall for that purpose and proceeded to shave. Gwen was still standing, hands behind her back, watching the damp buildings and the town where the new sun caused the rain's leavings to gleam like silver.

'You don't have to keep looking out the window,' Sage said to her as he positioned his razor.

'I didn't know how sensitive you were,' Gwen said, turning toward him.

'Not at all. I'm hardly a sensitive man,' he replied, shifting his cheek for the razor's downstroke.

'You hide it well, or you imagine that you are doing so,' was Gwen's reply. Sage didn't feel the obligation to answer that remark.

With the bristle off his jaw he dabbed his face dry with the towel and buttoned his shirt. Gwen watched him as if he were a strange, unpredictable animal.

'Well,' Sage suggested, 'what do you say we get some breakfast? Then we can talk about what to do with you.'

'Do with me?' Gwen was completely surprised. 'Why, I already told you — I'm continuing on to Trinity one way or another. I don't know what there is to discuss if it's not finding a way for you to just desert me here.'

'Gwen,' Sage said in a slow, firm voice. 'I know you would be stranded if I left you in this town, but I am telling you again: I'm riding a dangerous trail and in Trinity there's going to be trouble.'

'Yes, so you said.' She shrugged her narrow shoulders. 'But that's only after you get there, right? As soon as we hit town I can start looking for my maiden aunts. I'll be all right after that.'

'You have a lot of faith.'

'Yes, I do, and I have some in you as well. If Trinity is trouble for you, think of what the trail to Trinity could mean for me, traveling alone.'

Sage had been thinking of that. A lone woman, unarmed, with trouble on her trail . . . the situation stank. He finished buttoning his shirt and growled, 'Let's eat.'

Gwen only nodded and they exited the room, traipsing down the hallway of the still mostly asleep hotel. Breakfast was scrambled eggs and ham served in a low-ceilinged, kitchen-smoked restaurant by a surly waitress with drooping jowls. Maybe, Sage thought, they could have looked around and found a better place. But who knew, this might have been the finest establishment in Drovers' Springs. Besides it was more important to just jam some food down and hit the trail again early.

Sage was pleased and surprised to find a small but ripe fresh peach served for dessert. He stood now on the porch of the restaurant, nibbling at it. Beside him Gwen said little as she had said almost nothing over breakfast. Sage could tell she was anxious and uncertain.

'What's your plan?' Sage asked now, separating his business from hers. It wasn't that he disliked her, but she was an impediment to his goals.

'I've told you once or twice at least,' Gwen replied, her voice sounding a little snippy. 'I am riding on to Trinity to stay with my maiden aunts.'

'Your father will certainly miss you by now, he not even knowing where you have gotten to.'

'I will write him a letter from Trinity. He'll understand why I had to get away from the farm,' Gwen said, her voice still a little stiff. Sage felt as if he were letting the woman down, but then he had made her no promises, owed her nothing. She watched him as he silently munched on the juicy peach, wondering how the restaurant had come by it in this part of the country.

'Father once tried to grow peaches from good Georgia root stock, but the winters here are too cold, the summers too dry. Besides, the soil is not suited for them as it is in the South.'

Sage only nodded. He had stepped from the porch into the muddy street. The traffic was light. One ore wagon passed them by and a roaming cowboy, apparently lost, looked over the street from the back of his pinto pony. Gwen continued to chatter as they walked toward the stable. It seemed to be some nervous reaction to her uncertain circumstances. 'Besides there's not much that can be done with peaches except putting them up.'

'Peach pie is good,' Sage said, just so that Gwen would not think he was ignoring her. He was hoping that his gray horse's hock had recovered after a good night's rest. He needed to make better time than he had been.

'Yes, it is,' Gwen agreed, as they walked along, Sage obviously striding too rapidly for her. He slowed himself deliberately.

'What did your father want to do with them? And why did he give up on them? A few trees would be nice to have.'

'As I say, you can't do that much with them,' Gwen said, still hurrying along beside him, her eyes turned down, her face intent, 'unlike apples.'

'I don't see much difference,' Sage said, as they reached the plank walk across the street. 'Wouldn't Mr Kiebler be just as pleased to carry peaches as apples and cherries in his store?'

Gwen almost stopped in her tracks, turning to face Sage in front of a hardware store where a man was sweeping the walk.

'I never thought that you were such

an unobservant man, Sage Paxton,' she said, puzzling him.

'What are you talking about?' he asked a little gruffly.

'There's a lot than can be done with apples,' she said, now fixing her dark liquid eyes on his. 'Especially when the product can be smuggled on to an army post.'

'Product? Look, Gwen, maybe I am unobservant, but I still don't know what you're talking about.' She gawked at him as if he were the fool of all time.

'Do you know what applejack is?'

'Of course I do, though I don't favor it — hard cider, you mean.'

'That's right. Wouldn't you suppose there's more profit in that than in fresh fruit?'

'Of course there would be,' Sage admitted. They still had not moved along the plank walk toward the stable, Now as the sweeping storekeeper moved nearer, Sage nodded to the man and they stepped down into the muddy alley.

'You can't mean what you're saying,' Sage said. 'Your father is selling applejack to Kiebler, who sells it to the soldiers at Fort Vasquez?'

'Of course! Didn't you notice anything while you were loading Kiebler's wagon?'

Thinking back, Sage did remember thinking that some of those sacks of apples were awfully heavy. 'Kiebler would never sell liquor to the troopers. He told me so.'

'What would you expect him to say?' Gwen asked, a sort of pitying look on her face.

'It would cost him everything if Captain Rowland found out about it,' Sage objected.

'Sage,' Gwen said with a little shake of her head. They had halted beside a freight wagon which stood in the alley next to the stable. 'There's plenty of profit to go around.'

'You can't mean that Rowland knows all about it! That could cost him his commission.'

'Who is ever to find out?' Gwen asked. 'Rowland can always claim that he knew nothing about it. When there is to be a delivery, the captain is always conveniently away from the post.' Yes, well, he had been gone this time, Sage knew.

'I can't believe it,' Sage said.

'What? That men will break the rules if there's a profit in it?'

'But Kiebler said that he was dead-set against liquor being brought on to the post.'

'Again, what would you expect him to say? Confess all to a man he had just met?' Gwen shook her head. 'I like Mr. Kiebler — I happen to think he's a nice man, but then he is just a man who saw an opportunity to make a lot of money; Rowland, as well: the captain was probably raking in twice or three times a month what the army pays him.

'I'm starting to wonder about you, Sage. I believe you are an honest man, that is why the most transparent lie may not seem so to you.'

'I thank you for that, if it was intended as a compliment,' he replied.

'It was,' Gwen said, now smiling up at him, 'as awkwardly phrased as it was.'

'I've got to see about my horse,' Sage said, still a little miffed at Gwen's comment.

He stepped away from the parked wagon and started toward the stable doors, which is when the bullets from the unknown gunman began to fly around them.

6

The bellowing sounds of a .44 being touched off filled the alleyway, and wood exploded from the holes being bored into the wagon's side planks and whined off the metal brace straps. Taken completely unaware, Sage Paxton dove for the ground, slapping Gwen's legs out from under her to bring her down as well. Wriggling aside a little more, Sage glanced at Gwen to see that she was all right and simultaneously slicked his Colt from his holster.

Lying prone, peering into the shadows of the alley he could see nothing, no one. Gwen was clinging to his arm and he shook her off. There was nothing but the rolling clouds of black powder-smoke rising toward the clear sky and the insistent lingering echoes of the gun.

And then there was. Still peering from his position beneath the freight wagon, he caught sight of a man's legs as the attacker raced toward the foot of the alley. Sage triggered off three rapid rounds. His first shot flew wide, his second caught the man in the leg and, as he doubled up, Sage's third bullet caught him high on the shoulder. The gunman buckled to the damp earth, and Sage knew that it was over.

Gwen was gibbering meaningless sounds. Her hands were clawing at the earth, her face frantic. Her dark hair was now draped across her forehead and eyes.

'What happened?' she demanded in a shaky voice. 'Who was it?'

'I don't know. Stay here; I'm going to find out.'

Rolling out from under the wagon Sage approached the downed shooter cautiously, his Colt still in his hand. Gwen had come off the ground as well and she plodded along behind him in short, nervous steps.

'You don't mind very well, do you?' Sage asked.

'No,' she replied. 'I wanted to see who it was. Do you think it's Austin Szabo?'

'I don't know,' Sage answered. The gunman had been his first guess as well, but if it was Szabo he didn't deserve his reputation. The man had not been a good shot at all. He had not been more than fifty feet away when he had started firing, and he had missed with every shot.

As Sage suspected, the man was dead. The bullet he had taken in the shoulder had passed through and penetrated his upper ribcage, stopping his heart. Sage turned the man partly over with his boot toe and discovered that it was not Szabo who lay there. Gwen gasped.

'Do you know this man?'

'Yes,' she said shakily, 'it's Caleb Hornblower.'

'Who in blazes is Caleb Hornblower?' At the head of the alley a few men, drawn by the gunshots, had gathered, muttering among themselves.

'He worked for my father,' Gwen told him. 'He wasn't a very nice man.'

'What was he doing here?'

'Looking for us, I'd imagine. Can we get away from him now?'

'We'd better, I suppose. The law is bound to show up. If anyone asks neither of us knows who he was.'

'All right.' Gwen nodded solemnly.

'I've got to get my horse, Gwen. I don't intend to stay around this town any longer than we already have.'

Mutely she followed him back toward the stable. Sage said not a word to the gathered bystanders. To Gwen he hissed, 'How many others have you brought along to trail us?'

'Me . . . ? Sometimes you make it hard to like you, Sage Paxton,' she said, affronted.

'I don't need anyone to like me,' he said as they entered the barn under the curious stableman's gaze.

'A little trouble out there?' the man asked.

'The marshal can take care of it.'

'All right, then,' the man said, 'but — '

'How's my horse looking this morning?' Sage asked, ignoring the stableman's eyes and unasked questions as he walked to the stall where the big gray stood, Gwen's horse beside it.

He wasted no time in outfitting his gray. It showed no sign of continuing disability, which was for the better. Otherwise Sage, as much as he liked the animal, would have considered trading it off, and he hadn't the money for a good horse — not as good as the gray, anyway. He thought of purchasing supplies for the trail, but he was now halfway to Trinity, and he had no extra money. He contented himself with filling his canteens from the rain barrel outside the stable, which was overflowing with the recent rain, unhitching his mount, and emerging into the clear sunlight.

To find Gwen Mackay, already mounted, waiting for him.

'What are you doing here?' Sage demanded.

'I'm continuing on to Trinity, and we both agreed that it was not safe for me to travel alone out here.'

'We did? When was that?'

'We discussed it several times, Sage. Is your memory that bad?'

'No, but my mood is.' He yanked the gray's head around and started toward the west end of town. The crowd in the alley still had not dispersed which could mean that the town marshal had arrived to investigate. Sage wanted no one noticing him and lifting a pointing finger in their direction. He had had enough of Drovers' Springs and all he ever meant to see of it. He rode on, careful not to look back.

Soon they were out on the wide, red-soiled land, which was still slathered with rainwater which glittered dully beneath the sun hanging in the empty sky at their backs.

'They're not coming fast enough to be after us,' Gwen said.

'Who?'

'Those men on horseback behind us.'

'We must be well past the town limits,' Sage said, now looking back himself. He could see two, possibly three men trailing them.

'Does that mean they'll give it up?'

'It should, unless the marshal is the type who just doesn't like to give up — or unless they'll be happy enough not to try closing ground until after we're farther from town.'

'Why would they do that?' Gwen asked.

'It would save them the trouble of bothering with a trial,' he told her.

'I can't believe it,' Gwen said, turning her eyes back again. 'I think they've turned off or halted,' she said.

'Good. Let's not count on it, though.'

'Sage — some men spend their whole lives looking over their shoulders, don't they? How can they do it?'

'Beats me,' Sage grumbled, but he knew very well why. They had made crime the most important thing in their lives. And, Sage reflected, that was the way the rest of his life would be — if he was lucky enough to survive. But, retribution could not be withheld simply because of a fear of the consequences. Then Sage fell into a glum silence again, and Gwen felt that she had said the wrong thing once more, though she didn't know what that was.

They passed through a small oak grove and then out on to the seemingly endless land. Sagebrush and nopal cactus dotted the landscape, but nothing larger flourished there. Glancing at Sage Paxton, Gwen took a slow breath and then decided to ask the question that had been lingering in her mind.

'Well, Sage, it's a long trail ahead of us. Won't you tell me about it now?'

'Tell you about what?'

'About what's made you so angry. I can't believe you're normally like this. What has made you so determined to kill?'

'I can't see that it's any concern of yours.'

'I suppose it's not. That doesn't keep

me from wondering.'

'All right.' Sage looked for a long minute into the distance while his pony rocked under him. Finally he answered her. 'My parents have been murdered, and my brother is responsible.'

'Does he have a name?'

'Of course! I just dislike sullying my tongue with it; it's Brian. Brian Paxton. He's now the Marshal of Trinity.'

'My goodness,' Gwen said.

'I know. It's not clever to make a lawman your target. They'll hang you sure, to teach people to respect law and order.' Sage sighed, 'But that means nothing to me. I wouldn't care if he was the pope. I know what he did and he has to be punished for it, mortally punished.'

'How can you be so sure that Brian did it, were you there? What happened exactly?'

'Mom and Dad were at an age when minding the ranch just wasn't that appealing any more. They wanted to sell off the property and move into town someplace where things would be easier for them. Apparently they shared this thought with Brian, who was counting on assuming control of the ranch. Then they told him that it would be a year or two in coming, that they weren't quite ready yet. And there was the possibility of portioning the land with his brother.'

'You.'

'Me,' Sage nodded.

'It doesn't seem that should be too unexpected,' Gwen said. 'Parents try to be even-handed in seeing that everyone shares in their legacy.'

'No, it doesn't seem that unreasonable,' Sage agreed. 'I don't even know if I would have wanted to share the ranch with Brian — we didn't always get along that well. But Brian couldn't wait for two years, and he couldn't stand the thought of having to share with me. I was always away, concerned with various other endeavors like most young men of ambition. And there he was, laboring on the ranch day after day. As I said, I wasn't sure I wanted to go home again. Things hadn't worked out especially well for me. It would have been admission of failure.'

Gwen nodded as if she at least partly understood the rather complicated telling.

'If, to me, to return would have been an admission of my own inability, it was Brian's burning ambition to have the property for himself, and make some changes Dad was reluctant to make in his advanced years, and improve the land and the way business was done.'

He went on, 'Brian wanted everything, and he wanted it *now*. He bridled at laboring day after day, under Dad's restraints, for a cowhand's wages. Brian wanted to be a landowner and respected cattleman. And besides, he wanted the house to live in as he was courting Beryl and had virtually promised that it would be her bridal gift.'

'Who was Beryl?' Gwen asked, and watched as Sage's eyes hardened and he turned his face away.

'No one. Just Brian's new love.'

'I see,' Gwen said, understanding more from Sage's expression than she could have gleaned from his words.

'Then Brian made his move,' Sage continued. 'There was a fire in the house one night. Mom and Dad were savagely burned. Dad died instantly; Mom clung to life for a few days.'

'But why was it assumed that Brian was responsible?'

'It wasn't, not by the townspeople. But I knew. I knew because he was selfish: he wanted the land for himself and he wanted the house for Beryl so that she would agree to marry him.' Sage's voice was low, but far from calm.

'The fire scorched only one room of the house — my parents' room. It did not spread. So the damage to the house was not widespread. How could that happen? It was not some murderous passing vagrant. The dogs would have torn him apart. It had to have been Brian.'

'That's all you know of it — and that

all secondhand?' Gwen asked. 'I have told you before that I felt you were subject to hasty judgements — '

'I have other proof, positive proof,' Sage answered in a steely tone. 'There is the letter,' he said, withdrawing a much-folded piece of paper from his vest. 'Do you want to read it? It's from someone who knows what happened!'

Gwen declined the offer. 'Just tell me how anyone who was not there when the fire started could be sure,' she said. 'And tell me who the letter is from.'

'All right,' Sage said. 'It's from the one person who could know, someone who is sick at heart over it. It's from Beryl.

'She says that Brian arrived all smoky one night, burst in and told her that it was done; now they could be married.'

'Did they marry?' Gwen asked.

'No, of course not!' Sage answered, with a touch of indignation. 'Beryl is made of finer stuff; she couldn't wed a man who had murdered his own parents believing that he had done it for her.'

'And she wrote you all about this?'

'I was in Socorro, working on a deal to transport copper ore from the mine to the refinery. I'd been there for quite some time and meant to remain there until matters were settled. Beryl had been answering my parents' correspondence for them. She got my address off the envelope of a letter I had sent to Mom and Dad.'

'And she wrote to you to accuse your brother?' Gwen said, somewhat astonished.

'It was no good telling anyone in Trinity, was it? Brian had hired the judge's son as foreman of the ranch while he got himself appointed to the vacant town-marshal post. That must have been just to delay any real investigation.'

'You still have the habit of making too many speculative decisions,' Gwen commented. 'Have you given any real thought as to why Beryl would condemn your brother? Why would she write to you?'

'She knew that above anyone else I would demand retribution,' Sage said with certainty. 'Now you're the one making various assumptions, Gwen. That's because you don't know Beryl like I do.'

'You trust her that much?'

'I trust Beryl more than anyone on this earth. That's one of the reasons why I was going to marry her when I came back from making my fortune in the world.'

'You were engaged to her?'

'That's what I said, isn't it?'

'But — '

'But I was long out in the world and unsuccessful in my attempts to position myself. I suppose eventually her hopes for me and even her memories of me were bound to fade.'

'You would have been better off as a ranch owner,' Gwen told him.

'I've thought so too at times,' Sage admitted glumly.

'The need to do the right thing is what prompted her to write, not the promise of the ranch which if Brian were gone would then be entirely yours and the house?'

'I resent that implication,' Sage said harshly. 'It is not possible at all — not with a woman like Beryl.'

Gwen shrugged apologetically. 'It's only that I like to remain open to all possibilities. I'm not given to rash judgements.'

'Like me,' Sage growled.

Gwen didn't answer. Her eyes were fixed on the land behind them. She said, 'They've gotten closer again, and this time they appear to be coming with a purpose. The three of them have their rifles unsheathed.'

7

The riders behind them were coming in a rush and, as Gwen had said, there was murderous intent in the way they carried their rifles and spurred their ponies on. Who were they?

Men from the town intent on tracking down the killer of Caleb Hornblower? That seemed a good guess but also an unlikely one. No one there would have known or cared about Hornblower who was down from the Vasquez country looking for Gwen, and no one had shown any interest in their leaving as they rode out of Drovers' Springs. If the marshal there was the least bit observant, there was ample evidence that Hornblower had done his share of the shooting.

Could it be Austin Szabo? That was possible, Sage knew, but did Szabo have the necessary anger in him to ride this far chasing a runaway woman no matter that he had claimed Gwen as his own? There must be dozens more acquiescent women in the outlaw town of Barlow.

They hadn't seen Szabo back in Drovers' Springs, but that was where he would have made his play, it seemed to Sage. Szabo could have abducted Gwen there without even a fight or having to watch his back trail. Sage would not reverse course and ride back toward the Vasquez again pursuing them.

Sage had one other thought that was even less palatable: they were now nearer to Trinity than to Drovers' Springs. These men could have come from that direction, circled and come up behind them. Suppose Beryl had let something slip, or been angry enough to shout out a threat of Sage's wish to exact revenge on Brian Paxton. Suppose these men were a group sent out from Trinity to watch the trail for the returning brother of Marshal Paxton? If Brian did not mean to have it out face to face with Sage, the open country would be a good place to end it for good and all with him not even having to take a hand in things.

'See any badges on them?' Sage asked Gwen.

'No I don't — not at this distance,' she answered. 'They're still closing ground very quickly. What are we going to do, Sage?'

'Ride like hell,' Sage answered, yanking his own Winchester from its scabbard, for that was all that he could think of doing as the riflemen closed on them.

He slapped spurs to his big gray, glancing at Gwen to make sure she was doing the same, and then they were riding wild across the rough country. Sage looked around as they drove ahead, looking for some familiar landmark. He had, after all, lived his entire life or that which he could remember, in and around Trinity, at times riding far and wide, but the terrain all seemed unfamiliar. Had the passing of the years erased all memory of the land?

The men behind them had still not opened up with their guns. They seemed content to chase Sage toward Trinity town to encounter Brian wearing his new marshal's badge surrounded by a group of responsible citizens. There Sage's accusations would fall on deaf ears — a madman carrying mad tales.

Then any gunplay would certainly bring about Sage's death, whether under the guns of his brother and the townspeople or, if he were victorious, at the hands of the gentlemen of the jury. Sage's anger seemed no longer strong enough to support the sort of reckless fury that urged him madly on his way. The town must be avoided for the time being.

There was time to plan his face-off with Brian Paxton more fully later.

Sage dipped his horse into a ravine, and watched as Gwen plunged her bay pony down the sandy bank to join him. His gray horse was now limping under him again after the rigors of the run and the effort of scrambling down to the creek floor. Could it make it up the opposite bank? Sage thought it might not have to. He looked at Gwen, who sat her weary bay, her eyes wide with fear and doubt, looking up at the ravine's sandy opposite bluff.

'Are we going up there?' she asked.

'No. I don't think my horse can make it. There's another way to do this, and we might lose those men altogether if we take it.'

'What then?' Gwen asked and it seemed she was close to frustrated, weary tears.

'We're riding south,' Sage said grimly. 'I'm going home.'

They followed the meandering creek bed southward through sparse willow brush. There was only a trickle of running water; the rain that had fallen must have been diverted in a different direction. That was for the best. The travel on a weary, injured pony was difficult enough without the rush of a creek. Sage paused on two different occasions after they had rounded a bend in the wash, listening, but there was no sound as of onrushing horses. The loudest sound in the wash just then was an unhappy mockingbird scolding them as they passed disturbing his peaceful sunny morning.

They rounded another bend in the sinuous stream bed, passed under the low limb of a close-growing sycamore tree and found the land ahead widened and became flatter grassland. A single white-faced steer stood alone on a distant hillock displaying only bovine indifference to the two approaching humans.

Sage again halted his horse. His face now had a different expression, almost dreamy, Gwen thought. She waited patiently for a minute or two and then asked, 'What is it, Sage?'

'Home — I'm home again,' he told her.

To him that obviously meant a lot, but was it the healthy, natural pleasure of returning to home after long traveling, or the unbalanced pleasure of a half-crazed man nearing his desire: a killing ground?

'I think I can just see the house,' Gwen said, pointing in that direction.

'Yes, that's it.'

'A lovely setting,' Gwen said, admiring the view, the rolling land, the far mountains.

'Lovely setting for a murder,' Sage muttered. He had obviously done very little thinking about the points she had raised earlier — the possibility that Beryl had something to do with things, playing one brother against the other. Maybe he just refused to consider that.

He had described Beryl in almost saintly terms, as being loyal, fine, above perfidy. It was obvious that he was still in love with Beryl or her memory. It was equally obvious, to Gwen, that there was a very good chance that Beryl had gently prodded him into becoming a murderer for her sake. It seemed Beryl did not care which brother won, which was killed, so long as she got what she wanted. There was no point in bringing any of this up with Sage Paxton. He had painted his own image of Beryl based on his own wishes and desires. It was a portrait he would not allow to be criticized. He needed it to endure in his hall of memory for his own sake. Sage continued to show a tendency to cling to hastily made decisions. No, she thought, looking at his face as he leaned forward intently studying the land, there was no point in trying to get him to reconsider the few facts he had assembled into his jigsaw of reality.

To Sage there was only one way that the pieces fit. There was only the good: Beryl, who had cut her ties with Sage when he had not returned rich from his wandering merchant days, and the bad: Brian, who had murdered his own parents, stolen his woman and now must die for his crimes.

It was a brutal landscape Sage Paxton had assembled in his mind.

'Let's ride on down,' Sage said, having satisfied himself that there were no pursuing men behind them.

On the next rise he paused again and commented, 'I don't see many cattle. Wonder if Brian has been doing some selling-off.'

'There's someone you could ask,' Gwen said, lifting a finger to point out an approaching horseman.

Coming nearer to them, Sage squinted at the man on the chestnut horse, trying to make him out.

'He doesn't seem to be carrying menace,' Gwen commented.

'He's not showing it at least,' said Sage, who now had recognized the rider.

'Do you know him?' Gwen asked.

'It's Charlie Cable, Judge Warren Cable's son.'

'The man Brian hired as ranch foreman?'

'The same. Charlie's all right — just a little frosty around the edges. He spent his growing-up years where crime and criminals were a constant topic. It seems to have given him an untrusting view of his fellow man.'

Charlie Cable's expression was dry as he drew up facing them. His eyes shifted from Sage to Gwen and back again without changing expression. His eyes were a lawman's eyes, skeptical, alert for shadows of trouble. Gwen wondered if the judge's son wasn't cut out for that sort of work, more so than Brian Paxton, who, by all accounts, was a rancher to the core. But perhaps Charlie, tired of the talks of lawlessness he heard daily at home, shunned the very thought. Perhaps Judge Cable had wanted to avoid the appearance of favoritism. Perhaps Brian had simply shouldered his way into the job, giving Charlie Cable the ranch foremanship as a sop.

'I don't see many cattle grazing,' Sage said directly.

'Not up this way,' the sharp-featured judge's son agreed, tilting his hat back a little from his forehead. 'We've been slowly gathering the longhorns. We're keeping them separate these days. Brian has it in mind to cull them and bring on more shorthorns to replace them. He says the day of the longhorn is gone, and I have to agree with him.'

Gwen watched Sage's face, his eyes. She could see no reaction there, either of approval or disapproval.

'Is Brian down to town?' Sage asked.

'He was, the last I knew,' Charlie answered, his expression clouding.

'I guess I'll stop by the house before riding in there,' Sage said. Now Gwen could read his expression, and it was not a nice expression at all.

'As you like. This is the Paxton place after all. I got to see if we still haven't a few stray holdouts farther down along the creek,' Cable said, tugging his hat down lower again. He was obviously anxious to be away from Sage Paxton, back to his daily routine. Before walking his chestnut horse away, Charlie glanced once more at Gwen and then said, 'She's there, Sage. Beryl is down at the house.'

Then touching two fingers to his hat brim in a gesture of farewell to Gwen Mackay, the ranch foreman started his horse away from them. Gwen looked to Sage for an indication of what they were going to do now, but his expression was a glaze — not just his eyes, but his entire face seemed to be glazed over as if it had been dipped in lacquer and left to harden.

After another minute, Gwen prodded, 'Sage? What are we going to do?'

His answer was nearly a growl. 'What did I say we were going to do! Let's make our way down to the house.'

The front door to the house stood open, presumably to air it out. Gwen detected no scent of smoke as they crossed the front yard between four stately old black oak trees and approached it. She thought she could faintly smell lye soap and still more subtly the scent of bleach. Someone had been cleaning up, obviously.

Maybe she had been wrong about

Beryl, who, it seemed, must be the one who had volunteered to clean up after the fire. But then, it was Beryl who probably assumed that the house would be hers some day not now far away. Perhaps she was just making ready for ownership — no matter which brother should prevail in their duel. Brian Paxton had already proposed to her, and Sage, still carrying images of her in his mind, could be easily convinced that he was the only man she had ever loved.

'I wonder is she here,' he said, as they approached the hitch rail and swung down from their ponies.

'That's what Charlie Cable said.'

'No one's stirring about. She might have finished for the day and gone away.'

'Leaving the door open?' Gwen answered. 'You're just afraid to meet her, Sage.'

Sage's mouth tightened at Gwen's taunt. 'I hardly think that,' Sage said, a little too loudly, and he stepped up on to the porch. 'You're a nuisance, Gwen, you know that?'

'So I've been told,' she replied.

Gwen had been measuring the house from the outside. Of white, sawn wood it had two stories and in front of it a porch supported by four round pillars. Hardly imposing, it was nevertheless quite substantial for this part of the country.

Sage had tramped into the living room and Gwen followed, holding her hat. Sage waved a hand around the comfortably furnished room, at the native stone fireplace. 'Like it?' he asked. There was a little evident pride in his voice. 'It seems smaller than it did when I was a kid growing up here, but folks tell me that's a general impression kids going home always have. Really it's quite grand. I can still see my pa in shirtsleeves helping the carpenters with the rough framing, sawdust coating the entire house, Ma smiling as she tried to keep up with the sweeping.

'Pa kept telling her that the men could saw faster than she could clean up after them, and Ma laughed, admitting it. Before we moved in here, you see, we had an extended log cabin a little nearer to town and Ma was sick of it. She had such pride in her new house being built that she never went back to the cabin after the day she stepped inside here. Just kept on sweeping, spending the nights here. Her and Pa — I don't know where they slept; they hadn't gotten the new bed from Santa Fe yet. We kids — Brian and me — stayed back in the cabin where everything was familiar until the job was done.'

Sage's eyes remained reminiscent for long minutes. Well, after all, this was home to him and held a lot of memories, and no matter what he had said or hadn't said, Gwen thought that he was fond of this house himself.

'Sage!' the voice from the top of the interior stairs exclaimed. It was a woman's voice and Gwen looked that way to see the famous Beryl herself. Gwen watched her from a woman's perspective while Sage simply rushed toward the foot of the stairs, whipping his hat from his head.

Beryl wore a pale-blue dress with a little lace around the neck and at the cuffs. She was a very pale blonde with beautiful skin, a full mouth and wide, medium-blue eyes, all of which Gwen took in no less than Sage, who had rushed halfway up the stairs to escort Beryl to the living room.

'This is Beryl Courtney,' Sage said, as if the short run up the stairs had left him breathless. He had his hat in his hands, standing beside Beryl like a bashful schoolboy. Gwen nodded.

'Beryl, this is Gwen, my — ' He seemed to lose his voice suddenly. What was she?

'Traveling companion,' Gwen provided. Sage embraced the offered term.

'My traveling companion. Gwen has come to Trinity to stay with her aunts.' Beryl's mouth which had tightened as she first saw Gwen now softened again. She was watching Sage with appraising eyes, but Gwen saw no love light shining there.

Beryl seated herself on the long leather couch, inviting Sage to sit beside her. She now adopted a lady of the manor expression, which she figured herself for. Beryl had done nothing, said nothing to antagonize Gwen, but Gwen found herself not liking and mistrusting the woman. She continued to stand.

'I sure am happy to see you again,' Sage was saying. 'We should have a good long visit. Maybe after I get cleaned up I can take you out to dinner somewhere.'

'Why go out?' Beryl asked. Her smile seemed false to Gwen, but then she was already prejudiced against the beautiful blonde, and for no particular reason. 'I can make supper right here. I have all the makings. Brian can come over as well and we can all have a nice long conversation.'

Sage started to say something, and Gwen could see the anger rising in him. Settling himself he answered, 'All right, if it's not too much trouble. We can just talk things out right here.' Gwen glanced at his eyes, seeing in their depths that Sage wanted more than talk from his meeting with his brother. He seemed determined to ruin his own life, probably Beryl's as well and end Brian Paxton's. Surely Beryl Courtney must have had at least a notion of what Sage was up to, but she said nothing. Her smile was now a fixed expression.

This night might mean the end of all of her problems — one way or the other. Or was that only the way Gwen was reading her? But no matter how things worked out, tonight was set to be a savage one.

'I want to see where it happened,' Sage said, rising.

'Have your look. You know the way.' Beryl did not rise but sat, hands clasped, studying the floor. Gwen stood by while Sage, his face set, his eyes resolute, started down the hall toward where his father and mother had lived, presumably loved, and died.

He paused before the door, feelings of hatred, love, memory and death dueling within him. Taking a small breath, holding it, he entered the charnel room looking for something he might be able to recover, something that might convict a murderer.

8

Sage stood surveying the room from the doorway for a long time. The window was open a few inches, and a light breeze drifted through the room his parents had shared for those many years. He shook himself mentally; he was not there for the nostalgia. The room had been cleaned, aired and scented, but somehow it still smelled of ash and death, of evil.

His parents' wide bed with the carved oak headboard was still where it always had been. How had the bed not gone up in flames? There seemed to be a little fire damage on the headboard and, as he looked closer, the footboard too had been scarred by the heat, though someone had polished the worst of the damage away; Beryl no doubt.

The bed was made up covered by a

red comforter, trimmed at all edges with white lace. Sage winced. His mother would never have allowed such a coverlet on her bed. His father would have had it tossed out.

Crouching, Sage could see the heavy burn marks across the floor beneath the bed. No amount of polishing could remove these deep scars. Two of the walls had been newly papered, presumably to hide the damage, but had not caught flame. Sage ran a hand across the face of the walls. No, these were sturdy and stable.

The fire had been set only in one spot designed for a particular purpose: to kill the two inhabitants. He glanced at the ceiling, which still showed heavy smoke damage although it had been painted over in white.

This fire had been set with precise calculation to murder two innocent people in their bed and leave the rest of the house intact. That had required a lot of practical planning and time to devise. It had not been executed in the anger or hatred of a single reckless moment.

There had been only one other occupant of the house at that time. One trusted resident: his brother Brian. With renewed anger Sage turned away from the room. There was nothing more to be viewed in there, not after this length of time.

Yes, he and Beryl had to talk, and if Brian was there as well, so much the better. Beryl too must have been seething with bitterness and disappointment, but she said nothing as Sage returned to the living room to find both women in the positions they had held when he left the room. Beryl, on the long leather couch, blue eyes turned down sorrowfully, Gwen, standing near the fireplace, an emotion he could not decipher on her tight lips and in her dark-brown eyes.

'Do you like the way I redid our bed?' Beryl asked. Sage tried to smile as he shrugged. Whose bed was it? Who was intended to sleep there?

'We mustn't keep you any longer,' Beryl said, looking at Gwen as she rose. 'I'm sure you're anxious to get over to your aunts' house.'

'I'll take her along,' Sage said. 'I've got to find a place to clean up, maybe buy a new shirt.'

'But . . . ' Beryl looked just a little bit miffed. 'You can as easily take a bath here, Sage. As for shirts — I'm sure Brian has many if you didn't leave some of your own behind.'

'No, I'd better leave. You have a lot to do. Besides,' he said, positioning his hat, 'I want to talk to that lawyer — what was his name, Winston? — and the banker as well, see if there's anything about the legacy that they need me to sign to finalize matters.'

'There could be, I suppose,' Beryl said. 'Best to make sure everything is legal and above board.'

'I think so. What time are we going to eat?'

'Anytime around sundown,' Beryl replied. 'If you happen to run into

Brian you might remind him,' she added with no intent evident in her eyes. She then raised up on tiptoe and kissed Sage lightly on his cheek. Gwen, watching Sage's face, could see that he had taken that kiss as a promise. Possibly that was Beryl's intent; who knew?

Swinging aboard their horses, they trailed slowly from the yard, Beryl on the porch watching after them. Sage kept his eyes turned that way, started to wave, decided not to, and rode on.

After half a mile, Gwen asked him, 'Do you think this is wise — coming out here just before dark for supper?'

'It's probably safer for me than meeting Brian in town where there are so many eyes and ears. Trinity is his stronghold now that he wears a badge.'

Sage's attention seemed to drift and they dipped into a shallow little valley surrounded by pine trees, the grass there lush and green. Gwen noticed his demeanor and asked quietly, 'What are you thinking about now, Sage, or do I even have to ask?'

'What are you talking about?'

'I mean it comes wrapped in lace.'

'Shut up,' he growled.

'Nice way to talk. All I meant was — '

The rifle shot cracked out from the forest verge above them, the thunder of its echo rolling across the valley. Gwen had time to think, 'I thought we were through with all of that,' before she was heeling her pony to follow the racing Sage toward the treeline.

She had time to mumble something similar to Sage as he swung down from his gray, snatching for his Winchester.

'Why would you think that? This is only the beginning of it. Haven't you been paying attention?'

They remained unmoving, silent for long minutes as the breeze whispered past, swaying the tips of the tall trees. Finally Gwen felt compelled to ask, 'Are you going after him?'

'In the timber when he knows where we are and we haven't glimpsed him?

That would be just a little reckless, don't you think?'

'I suppose, but who . . . ?'

'I don't know who. I . . . we . . . have made a few enemies lately, but this doesn't seem to match their patterns.'

'Can she shoot? Beryl, I mean.'

'Don't be ridiculous. Just because you don't like her.'

'Who said I didn't like her?'

'You were practically shouting it with your eyes.'

'I'll have to keep them more quiet,' Gwen answered. 'Where are we going to go? We have to get away, don't we?'

'We can make it to the old cabin — it's not far from here. Just keep to the timber, off the valley floor.'

'All right. Whatever you say; I don't wish to be pinned down here as we are.'

Neither did Sage. Swinging into the gray's saddle, he led Gwen northward toward where his old family home stood in splendid isolation among the pines. No passing stranger would be likely to stumble across it.

There was a good part of the day remaining yet, but Sage doubted he would have time to accomplish all he had meant to that afternoon. He needed to get Gwen to her aunts' home first. He wanted her out of the way before more serious shooting began. The lawyer, Winston, and the banker could wait. All of that might be irrelevant by sundown.

Emerging from the trees before Gwen had expected it, they came upon a long low log building. It had been built in two sections, the smaller, square structure first, the longer addition later when the one-room cabin had gotten too small for more than two people.

Eventually this, too, seemed not large enough for the new family, Gwen guessed, and they had begun the white house.

She could read nothing in Sage's eyes but he must have had long memories of this place.

They approached the front of the house and Sage swung down, entering the cabin with his hand close to his Colt. He leaned back out and beckoned to Gwen. She walked in, expecting to find the place musty, cobwebbed, long deserted, but the floors had all been swept and the furniture, old as it was, was clean.

'Someone's staying here,' she said in a whisper.

'Probably Brian when he's not in town overnight. He wouldn't have wanted to go back to the big house until it was polished up. Or,' Sage said, scratching his head, 'it could have been given over to Charlie Cable now that he's foreman of the ranch. His father's place is quite a way away. He might not have wished to stay with his father anyway.'

'Possibly not,' Gwen, who knew nothing of Cable's relationship with his father, the judge, replied. 'The question now is, how long do we stay here and where are we going next?'

'Straight to your aunts' house. I'm hoping you know where it is.'

'Someone will tell us,' Gwen answered.

'You don't know, then?'

'I've never been to Trinity, Sage! And as you know, this wasn't exactly planned.'

'We'll find it. All I want to do in the meantime is wait here until we're sure no one's following us. If they are, this is a better place to stand them off than being out in open country.'

'You're thinking about those three men who were following us.'

'I'm thinking of those three men, whoever they were. I'm thinking of the marshal from Drovers' Springs. I'm thinking of Austin Szabo and his Barlow crowd. I'm thinking of my brother and whatever loyal friends and deputies he might have assembled,' he said irritably. 'Have I forgotten anyone?'

'Just Charlie Cable and . . . her.'

'Neither one of them makes any sense,' Sage snapped.

Gwen turned her back and answered, 'Then I guess you haven't forgotten anyone, and it's quite a large enough crowd for me.'

'For me too,' Sage said in a voice that was slightly apologetic. He walked to the front window and stood peering out. 'We'll give it a half-hour and then be on our way. The sooner we get you to Trinity, the happier I'll be. You'll be safer there.'

'You think my aged aunts are a match for Austin Szabo?' she asked in a tone Sage didn't care for.

'It's not him,' Sage barked, half turning from the window. 'No one's chasing you now. You'll be perfectly safe in Trinity, and I'm more than a little tired of being responsible for you. The facilities are around back if you need them,' he said. He then returned to his watching.

No one, nothing stirred near the cabin or among the concealing pines for a good half an hour, and so Sage decided it was time to move if they were to get anywhere with what was left of the day.

'We can go now,' he said to Gwen.

'Is it safe?'

'Who can ever tell, but yes, I think it is.'

'Well,' Gwen said with a sigh, rising from the couch with some reluctance. 'Let's be going.'

'What's the matter with you? You want to get to Trinity, don't you? To your aunts' house.'

'I suppose so,' Gwen said.

'You *suppose* so. Woman, I've put quite a bit of time and effort into getting you here,' Sage said in a low voice.

'I know it, but Sage . . . that's not my home either, is it?'

'Well, you had a home and you left it.'

'You know why,' Gwen said a little sharply. Her dark eyes flashed. 'By now I'd be living in Barlow with Austin Szabo if I hadn't found a way out.'

'You'll be all right now, much better off.'

'I suppose so . . . if they'll even take me in.'

'They're your mother's sisters. They'll take you in,' Sage told her.

'Maybe so. Sometimes old people are a little protective about their privacy, rigid in their habits.'

'That's why a good guest follows the rules of the house. You can abide by that for a while — you don't have to remain there forever.'

'No, I can go off on my own . . . I have so many talents.'

'You raise a fine apple,' Sage said, trying to lighten the girl's concern. She was worried, no doubt about it, as they approached the end of their trail. It seems that's the way most of us are. Distant dreams are somehow more strongly clung to than those approaching faster than we are prepared for.

'It'll be all right,' Sage repeated. He had the door to the cabin open now, peering out into the silence of the forest. 'Now, let's get moving. The end of our long trail is at hand.'

Sage referred to himself as well. The end of his long trail to Trinity had been reached. He, like Gwen, had to now face up to what that meant. His hate, focused on a man who was far distant, had been much stronger somehow. Now that he was in Trinity, still intent on putting lead into the familiar form of Brian Paxton, his brother, playmate and confidante of his youth, it seemed more than a challenging idea. It had descended to the distasteful. It was now not a heated thirst for vengeance, but a painful, dark plot that must be carried through.

The patch of woods fell away as they entered the red, open country that surrounded the town of Trinity, Colorado. The town had grown some since his last visit, before he had ridden away to find fame and fortune and blundered into one dead end after another . . . He had to keep talking. Brian was on his mind.

'Where did you say your aunts' house was?' he asked Gwen. She glanced at him quizzically.

'I've already told you — I don't know. I've never been to Trinity before.'

'All right. We'll find it — before dark, I hope. They'll be more apt to welcome company.'

'You can hardly wait, can you?' Gwen asked, her eyes turned away.

'For what?'

'To get rid of me, to stash me away somewhere so you can go about your important work: killing your own brother and recapturing the maiden.'

'You have a funny way of looking at things, Gwen. I said I'd take you here, and I did. I don't know what else you expect of me.'

'I don't either. Somehow all the way here, a small part of me believed that you'd come to see the utter futility of what you were planning on doing: killing a town marshal, your own brother, for which they'll surely execute you if you do come out ahead in the fight. I thought I saw your determination wavering just a little, but that was before you saw her again. A woman whom you cannot win at all. Either you'll be dead or you'll be asking her to take up the outlaw trail with you — knowing her, that's totally impossible, and you know it. *What* are you going to win, Sage?'

'That's not what this is about,' Sage said, as they approached the town limits of Trinity. 'It's a debt that must be collected in blood.'

'I'm sure you'll be happy as soon as you've done that — no matter that Brian might not have even been responsible. You haven't even given him a fair trial, a chance to explain — Here are some people; let's ask them if they know my aunts.'

Since Gwen did not even know the main streets of the town to take reference from, Sage did the talking to the farmer and his son they stopped. Nodding, Sage started his horse again. To Gwen he said, 'I think I can find it.'

They rode on, turning away from the heart of town. Gwen was silent in her saddle, her eyes distant. Sage, too, rode silently. The burnish of his righteous mission of retribution seemed to be fading as the glow of the sunset sky briefly brightened and then fell away toward darkness.

The cross street was Elm, which Sage knew. Once outside of town, it petered out into two roughly sketched dirt trails, unnamed, which forked in different directions. 'This way,' Sage said, nodding to his right, toward a trail which seemed to be the lesser used.

'Are you sure?'

'No, but the farmer said keep to the right, and that's this way.'

Gwen seemed uncertain, but it was not doubt about their direction that caused it. The girl seemed unwilling to reach her goal, to finally find the end of the long trail to Trinity. He urged her forward. 'Come on, they can't be as bad as all that.'

Her eyes shifted toward him, damp and questioning in the faltering light of the day. 'No,' she muttered, heeling her horse forward, 'they can't be.'

What was troubling her? Sage had a dim inkling but he roughly shoved the notion aside. There was no point in even giving it any consideration. None of it would matter by tomorrow anyway, once his mission was done.

They continued along the dry road past bare hills until they crested out overlooking a small valley where a stream trickled past. The house standing there was quite small — Sage guessed the place could have only one bedroom. It was a white, peeling little structure with two white oak trees standing in front of it. The house looked impoverished, but not entirely untended. The picket fence around it was either new or freshly painted. There were flowers growing along the front of the house. Right now these were being tended by a woman in a faded dress. She was quite small, frail-appearing. She turned a worried, birdlike head toward the arriving riders. Sage didn't imagine the two sisters had much company out this way.

'Is that one of your aunts?' Sage asked Gwen. The girl shrugged.

149

'I don't know, how would I know? I haven't seen them since I was a small girl. All I remember about them was that they were large.'

'Like that?' Sage asked, as a second woman emerged from within, drying her hands on her apron as she stood squinting in their direction. She was quite stout. Her face showed the lines of care, deeply carved. The two seemed of an age, though the one in the garden patch had been selected to waste away in her older years, the other to add layers of fat to her round body.

'I think . . . ' Gwen said hesitantly, 'I think I recognize her. That might be Aunt Alice. I'm almost sure it is. The other one would be Penelope.'

'You'll find out for sure in a few minutes.'

'Oh, Sage, what am I to do now?'

'It's simple. What you do is swing down and ask them if they have a niece named Gwen. After that whatever you feel like sharing about your situation is up to you.'

Gwen looked close to panic. Then, resolutely, she got down as Sage sat his horse, watching. He heard a few low, explanatory words from Gwen, a couple of murmuring responses from the aunts. Then they turned to hustle her into the house. Gwen halted at the doorway, lifting a hand toward Sage. She seemed to want to say something, but she turned and silently entered the house with her aunts.

Sage waited for another minute before he turned the big gray's head back to the south, toward Trinity which would be waiting in the solemn sunset, settling down for its evening rest.

Sage rode that way with cool deliberateness. He meant to rouse the town, or at least a good part of it, out of its sleep.

9

Trinity was still awake at this hour. When Sage reached the town limits there was still enough light to see by, though a purple shadow seemed to have been drawn over the town.

Lanterns burned behind a few windows where a shopkeeper was working late and other honest men went about their work. The bank he passed was closed; such establishments do not favor being open after dark.

The rifleman they had encountered along the road had delayed them just enough to cause Sage to miss talking to the banker concerning the will of his mother and father; however, riding his gray along the main street at a walk, he saw a shingle hanging from the eaves of an office, a light burning within the building. The sign and the painted legend on the front window both proclaimed it to be the office of Wilbur J. Winston, the very man Sage had hoped to see.

Tying his gray at the hitch rail, Sage rapped on the door and entered. Behind a desk a startled-looking man with a bald head and a Van Dyke beard looked up, pen poised over some papers in a stack in front of him.

'I'm closed for business,' the man said, in a somewhat surprising deep, husky voice.

'Aren't you Mr Winston?'

'I am, but I told you . . . Who are you? You look almost familiar.'

'The name is Sage Paxton, Mr Winston. I'm here to ask you about my mother and father's will.'

'I see.' He scribbled something on the paper before him, probably his signature, and placed the stack of the other papers aside. Winston leaned back in his chair and folded his hands together. 'What exactly is it you wish to know, Mr Paxton?'

'Just the general terms,' Sage said,

seating himself in a wooden chair across from the lawyer. 'I've never seen the will. There's that, and I wondered if there were any papers that needed my signature.'

'There's nothing you need to sign,' Winston said, peering closely at Sage. 'The will was legally signed and witnessed. I know that since it was done here in my office. Unless you are meaning to contest some of the will's terms, it is considered to be fully executed.'

'I have no reason to challenge the will or its terms.' Not with pen and ink, anyway. 'I just wanted to know if my understanding of it is correct — as I said, I never saw the actual will.'

'Surely someone would have written you.' Winston looked a little baffled. Sage was quick to respond.

'I was notified, but it was long afterward. I have been a traveling man and my letters take a while to catch up with me.'

'I see,' Winston answered, picking at

one tooth as if it was bothering him. 'It was quite a straightforward document with no special exemptions or exclusions of any sort. I can find my copy in a matter of minutes if you would like to study the full document.'

'I don't think that's necessary if you can recall the general terms. As I said, I was notified, but the information was second-hand, and my informant may have been mistaken on certain points.' Though Sage doubted it, Beryl was nothing if not a careful woman.

'Well, if you will agree to trust my memory, which is very good, I assure you, the cash — of which there was little, really — the house and the land with all of its assets — which I suppose must mean cattle — were to be divided equally between you and your brother, Brian. That's about all there was to it.'

'Was there anything about one of us predeceasing the other?' Sage asked. Winston blinked with surprise, then answered.

'That is a standard conditional clause

in all wills. If one or the other of you predeceased the other, the property ownership would fall to the other brother.'

'Yes. What would happen to it if neither of us were to survive?' which was directly to the point of the matter as far as Sage was concerned, but seemed to puzzle the lawyer again.

'The ranch and all of its appurtenances would then fall to the alternate heir, Miss Beryl Courtney — is that a disputable point with you, Mr Paxton?'

'No, not at all. That is the way my parents would have wanted it. It's the way both my brother and I would have preferred it.'

'You have discussed this with your brother, then?'

'Not yet,' Sage said, rising from his chair, 'but don't give it another thought, Mr Winston. Brian would agree with me on that point. I just wanted to make sure I understood how things had been arranged.'

'Well, that's it, so far as I recall,'

Winston said. 'If you have any further questions you are welcome to examine the entire document when you have the time.'

'That won't come up,' Sage said, putting on his hat. 'I know all I need to know about matters. And I won't be having much time in the immediate future.'

Winston's mouth twitched with a strange little bunched movement of his lips, either because of his tooth, or because he knew that whatever Sage had been trying to find out, it had been answered only incompletely. With a sigh he returned to his legal briefs as Sage crossed the small office and departed into the night.

All right, Sage was telling himself, that was taken care of. Beryl would be cared for no matter what happened on this night. Sage could not forecast the events; he only knew that it would end with blood being spilled in the town of Trinity.

Leading his gray horse then he began

walking along the street toward the marshal's office. He had gone no more than twenty paces when the first bullet rang out from a crossing alley, whipping his hat from his head. Sage dropped and rolled beneath his steady gray horse, unloosed his Colt and returned fire into the alleyway, the only possible place the ambush could have had its origin. His shots drew a pair of answering bullets. One of these struck his saddle pommel, and the gray, calm and stoic before this, started away, leaving Sage exposed in the middle of Main Street.

He was peripherally aware of people rushing toward him, of lights going on, and shouts being raised all along the street, but had no time to pay this much attention. There were still bullets flying around — only luck, the poor light, and possibly the ambushers' overeagerness had kept him from being tagged by spinning lead. With his horse gone, there was no escape. Defensively Sage threw himself to the ground, hoping to provide a narrower target silhouette for his attackers. From his belly he looked more closely into the dark alley. One man, he saw as a gun flashed in the darkness, had taken a position behind an outside stairway which Sage remembered as leading to the second storey of the dry goods store where women could try on dresses in privacy. He aimed his Colt as carefully as possible from his prone position and triggered off in that attacker's direction. His shot drew an eerie answer from that quarter. A shriek like a woman's scream raised itself into the night and, as it lowered in tone, continued as the low-voiced grumbling of a man cursing in pain.

On the heels of that a second gun opened up in Sage's direction, this one spattering him with roughly driven sand from the alley floor. Sage was able to shift his eyes that way to locate the second shooter squatted down behind a barrel. He fired one bullet at that ambusher.

At the same time the first gunman

rose from behind the staircase and ran toward the far cross-alley. Sage shot at this one again, and the man fell immediately to the ground, clutching his thigh.

The men behind Sage were drawing much closer in an angry knot. These could be associates of the men in the alley — there was no way of telling. He didn't know the motivation of any of the men, who they were. Perhaps the whole town had been riled by the return of Sage Paxton. He knew that he could not face that large a body of men — knew also that he could not go forward. One of his attackers was down; did that leave one man, or two, or . . . ?

Sage knew he had to leave or be gunned down like a dog from ahead or from behind. That would mean scraping himself off the ground and charging in the only direction he could take: straight ahead toward his ambushers. He would be offering a much better silhouette to shoot at, and this one would be approaching them. Behind him he could still hear the angry, arguing, cursing mob nearing.

Sage loosed another bullet from his revolver at the man behind the barrel to keep his head down, and rushed toward him, keeping to the far side of the alley. He could clearly see the man he had shot in the leg, sitting on the ground. Sage's assailant still had his pistol in his hand. He saw the murky shape of the second man behind the barrel.

And a third man who had appeared at the head of the alley, braced and ready for a fight. Sage was fired at again by the man behind the barrel. This shot tore into the planking beside Sage's head, spraying splinters. He fired that way carelessly. He realized only now that an earlier decision not to try to reload his Colt in the middle of things might prove to be fatal.

The third man fired as Sage tried to swerve past him, but the bullet was not aimed at Sage but at the attacker behind the barrel. Strange, Sage had time to think, before the jolt of impact stopped him nearly in his tracks, sudden darkness closed over him and he could feel himself tumbling to the cold hard floor of the alley, his night's quest brought to an abrupt and futile end.

* * *

'I think he's waking up,' Sage heard through the confusion of his tangled thoughts.

'I told you he'd be back among us soon,' a nearly familiar voice answered.

'With that goose egg on his head, I wondered,' the first man replied.

'Sage Paxton has too thick a skull to be bothered by something like that for long.'

'It must run in the family.'

'I suppose it does,' the other one answered with a short laugh.

Slowly Sage pried his eyes open. There was a terrific throbbing in his head. Peering through the pain toward the men conversing he saw the source of the nearly familiar voice. His face was instantly recognizable.

Brian Paxton had always had curly blond hair. Now he wore it nearly to his shoulders. A marshal's shield gleamed dully on his shirt front as he leaned back in a chair behind the jailhouse desk. He had also sprouted a blond mustache, neatly trimmed, which sprawled the length of his smiling upper lip.

Sage's brother was a handsome man, and he briefly resented him for it.

Realizing now where he was, Sage struggled to sit up. He was on a cot supported by chains in the narrow jail cell. The door to the cell stood open! That did not matter to Sage just then. He doubted he could make it to the cell door, let alone attempt to flee the marshal's office. Anyway he did not wish to flee from his brother — they still had not had their long talk. Sage had not even been disarmed, though reflecting he was not certain that there was even a single load left in it after the hasty hell of the alley shoot-out. He was just then a useless man with a useless Colt in a jail run by his brother.

Nothing seems to go according to plan.

'Are you awake, Sage?' Brian called out as if nothing were wrong between them. Sage didn't so much as grumble a response. The second man, a lean man in black Sage took for a deputy marshal, chipped in, 'He's sitting up, isn't he? He must be. It might be he left some of his brains out in the alley.'

'Where'd they get me?' Sage asked, speaking for the first time.

'You mean where'd you get yourself?' the deputy cracked. Sage frowned at the man. He had never liked being the butt of a joke, especially when he did not understand the gist of it.

'Knock it off, Harvey,' Brian Paxton said, rising to his feet behind his desk. The deputy, Harvey, nodded, muttered an apology, and shrugged, though he was still smiling.

'What happened to me?' Sage asked his brother, who had walked toward the cell to look down at him. 'I'm a little hazy on that.'

'They jumped you as you passed the alley — three of them, although the only one I recognized in the dark was the one you got. A local no-good named Bob Brown.'

'Who was he working for?' Sage asked, since it no longer seemed that his brother could have been involved in this. Sage sat on his hard bunk, head hanging as he waited for Brian's answer. He considered that he must have made a dismal sight just then.

'Bob Brown was no longer in any condition to tell me, being dead,' Brian said, with a faint smile. 'I'd only be guessing if I said anything, but I think it's the same crowd that's been after me.'

After Brian? Sage shook his fuzzy head, but all that did was bring a rising jolt of pain into his battered skull. 'What happened to me, Brian?' he asked after another minute's confusion.

'Knocked yourself out good and

proper,' Harvey said almost gleefully. Sage's troubles seemed to be amusing the deputy greatly.

'You glanced back at the man behind the rain barrel and ran yourself right into those outside stairs at the mercantile.'

Sage made a low, muffled sound. 'Hell of a way to end a glorious battle.'

'It probably kept you alive,' Brian commented. 'I went there to break up a gunfight. I couldn't identify anyone in the darkness. I saw you go down, the man behind the barrel flee — there were too many citizens at the head of the alley for me to risk firing that way again — and I crouched down to see if I could identify you.'

'And you did.'

'And I did. You didn't seem to have been hit so we dragged you over here and tucked you in to see if you were going to regain consciousness anytime soon.'

'Which I almost have. Brian, as you said, there was quite a crowd of men at the head of the alley, trying to see what was happening. All those men . . . didn't someone recognize the man behind the barrel as he ran out?'

'No one's come forward, but then a man waving a gun can make his way quickly through a crowd. And it was dark. He might not even have been a local man.'

'You think you know who it might have been?' Sage asked.

'I don't know if they weren't local guns. The reason I think they were imported toughs is because you showed up just tonight. Someone might have been asking around about where they could find Paxton, and someone pointed at you. Newly arrived gunnies might have assumed that you were me.'

'Could be, I suppose,' Sage said, 'but it seems a little unlikely.'

'Maybe it is, Sage,' Brian Paxton said, pursing his lips, 'but then a lot of unlikely things have been happening around Trinity lately.'

'You say someone wants you dead. Tell me, Brian, who would that be?'

'That?' Brian answered. 'Well, that one's pretty easy to answer: Charlie Cable, of course.' His eyes flickered toward Sage. 'And Beryl,' he added, as their eyes met.

10

'Beryl . . . ?' Sage tried to blink away the shock and confusion crowding his thoughts. Had he brained himself that hard? 'What do you mean Beryl might have had it done? Why would she? Aren't you two about to be married?'

'In her mind we are. I started to wonder about things after she told me that you had written her a letter in which you said you had determined to ride to Trinity and kill me.'

'I never wrote any such letter,' Sage protested, although he had definitely planned to do just that.

'What did you do?' he asked Brian.

'Do? What was there to do? I thought about it, decided that I knew you better than that. Why would my own brother decide to kill me?'

Perhaps because he had been told that Brian had murdered his parents

— by Beryl. Perhaps because he was stupid, filled with the wish for vengeance and still prompted by the memory of a beautiful woman and all that she could offer — in dreams.

'I was told that you killed Mother and Father,' Sage finally admitted.

'Told . . . ? By whom?' Brian's eyes showed concern now.

'Take your best guess.'

'Beryl.' Brian Paxton shook his head sadly, heavily. 'Sage, I wasn't anywhere near the ranch on the night that happened. I swear to you.'

'You don't have to, Brian, I believe you.'

'I've been looking for the killer ever since,' Brian said. 'Now, it seems I don't have to. Not any more.'

'She couldn't have done that — she can't be that evil!'

'You still think not, after she deliberately gave each of us a reason for killing the other and then brought us together?'

Sage said dully, 'I was supposed to

170

invite you out to supper tonight — after dark.'

'That would have wrapped things up neatly, the mood you were in.'

'And if it didn't work out the way she wanted it, I suppose she would have someone waiting to take care of us so that it would look like a shoot-out between us as she intended.'

'No doubt about that,' Brian said. 'I would bet anything that Charlie Cable was also invited to supper.'

'Why Cable?'

'The judge's son was kicked out of his father's house and needed to find a place to spread his wings. He had no way of making a living so he turned to petty crime. I'm aware of some of his transgressions though I never had enough evidence to arrest him. He hated me for that, for being the town marshal — a job he thought his father would hand to him — and for owning a half-interest in a working ranch. And for Beryl, who hired him over my objections.'

'He wanted her?' Sage asked.

'Doesn't every man she's ever met? Cable drifted that way, decided he had the right to what was mine. He brought in a few of his outlaw friends to try having me killed in Trinity when he could be on the ranch, far away from town. Some of those people are still hanging around, trying to claim the bounty Cable put on my head; Bob Brown, for example.'

'Couldn't none of them shoot from a distance,' Harvey said from across the room, 'and not a one of them had the heart to stand up to the marshal face to face.'

'I've had some success dodging their bullets,' Brian Paxton said, 'but it has made my life a little . . . uncomfortable.'

'So you think that Beryl decided to send for a man who would stand up face to face with you — me?'

'It seems likely, don't you think?' Brian said with a sigh.

'I think it's more than likely,' Sage answered.

'I was only counting on you not being so hot-headed that we wouldn't even have the chance to talk before you forced a fight,' Brian said, now studying his brother's eyes with sadness.

'To plan all of this for the hope of a house. She could have had the house, the ranch and all the income it brings in without any of this — without murder.'

'She couldn't be sure of that, Sage. And Beryl always wants to make sure.'

'My God!' Sage breathed softly. Then, looking up at the marshal, he said, 'You know, I have a friend who had this all figured out, and told me to be careful, to at least talk to you first before I rushed in headlong and made the biggest mistake of my life — and I didn't listen to her. I couldn't believe it of Beryl. She even explained that to me — said I couldn't see past the lace and the dreams.'

'What do you think now?' Brian asked.

'I think that was one smart little

woman I happened to meet on the trail to Trinity.'

'Seems so. I'd like to meet her someday if she's still around.'

'She should be,' Sage replied. He was thinking of the rough way he had guided Gwen to her aunts' house and dropped her off like an unwanted dog so that he could be free to resume his grand scheme.

'My question,' Sage went on, 'is what do we do now?'

'Well, you'll have to wash your face before we go, but I think the only right thing to do is ride on out to the ranch. After all, when someone is good enough to invite you to supper, you should at least show up.'

'It'll give Beryl a heart attack,' Sage answered. 'At least one of us is supposed to be dead by now.'

'They'll still have their chance. I told you I'd bet my last nickel that Charlie Cable is there waiting for Beryl to serve dessert.'

'So you mean for both of us to just

ride up to the front door as if nothing's wrong.'

'That's what I mean,' Brian Paxton answered. 'As of now there's not enough evidence to arrest Beryl for anything. Maybe she will provide us with some.'

'You're a bold man, Marshal Paxton,' Sage said.

'Look who I was learning from, growing up.'

'All right,' Sage agreed after a moment's hesitation, 'show me where I can wash up and let me reload my Colt. I think I may be needing it on this night.'

'I can almost guarantee it,' Brian answered, and he led Sage to a small back room which served as the lawmen's cupboard where a basin, ewer and almost-clean towel rested on a small stand.

'Want me to go along, Marshal?' a not-so-eager Harvey asked as they were leaving.

'No, I need you around town to try

keeping things peaceful. However, if you'd follow us along for a little way and make sure there are no uninvited guests trying to follow us, I'd appreciate it.'

'All right, I can do that,' Harvey agreed. 'Boss, eat with one hand on your Colt.'

Brian Paxton grinned without answering. Within a quarter of an hour they were riding south, Sage reunited with his gray horse, which had been taken to the stable after the shooting, Brian Paxton on a strutting four-year-old bay. Sage glanced at his brother with some family pride. He was a striking figure in the night with his long blond hair curling across his shoulders.

'You seem to have taken to the town marshal's job well,' he said, as they entered the long valley with sunset tinting the western sky to purple above the deep ranks of pines.

'Well enough, I'd say,' Brian answered across his shoulder as the high-stepping bay horse pranced along across the long grass of the valley floor. 'It was daunting the first week or so, but you know how it is, every job takes a little breaking in. I like it well enough. Up until this recent trouble the job was treating me fine. Lately I've been searching each stranger's face, watching every shadow. I don't like living like that, Sage.'

'Let's end it tonight, Brian. Have we a plan?'

'There's really none possible, is there? We'll go in and visit with Beryl, see how that twists up her able tongue and then wait and watch for a signal — there will have to be some kind of a signal.'

'You think the gunman — Cable or whoever it is — will be alone?'

'We can only hope. I don't see why they would have thought they needed more men. Only one of us was supposed to return to supper this evening.'

Sage nodded and tried to reposition

his hat. The knot that had developed on his skull made it hard to fit it comfortably. He was wondering how Gwen Mackay was doing on this night. Probably she had eaten with her aunts, exchanged a few tales, and gone to bed early, old folks not generally being night owls. He had some guilt nagging at his conscience concerning Gwen. Why that should be, he did not know.

He had done everything he had promised, helping her escape from the Vasquez country, seeing her safely home to her aunts. Still, he had not treated her kindly at times, and he knew it. She had only been a person to be gotten rid of. Just then she seemed like a girl he should never have let go.

He could see the shoulder of the big white house now in the murky light of evening. He paused for a minute, holding up his horse as did Brian Paxton. Without having discussed it they sat their ponies together, searching the land around them, watching for any shadowy movement, listening for any small, intruding sound in the dusk.

Starting on, they neared the house and Sage said, 'Big, isn't it?'

'Certainly too big for any one man,' Brian replied. 'You know, Sage, Mother didn't really want it.'

'What do you mean? I thought it was her dream.'

'No,' Brian said, shaking his head. 'She told me about it once years later. Father felt guilty about her having to live in log cabins while they struggled through the early years, and after the ranch started to grow and he was making more money, he decided to spend some of it on building his wife a grand home.'

'She always acted as if she loved the house — I remember her insisting she stay in it even while it was still being built.'

'Yes, she did, but it was Father's great gift to her after all of the suffering that had gone before. She knew his intentions and proceeded to make out that it was the finest gift a man could have given her. That gave Father a reason to remain proud; he had made Mother happy.'

'They were a grand couple, weren't they? They'd do anything to make each other happy.'

'Anything,' Brian agreed. 'That's the way it always should be, but so seldom is.'

There was a lantern burning in a front window and they guided their horses toward the hitch rail. Through the flickering shadows, they stepped on to the front porch and knocked on the door.

Beryl Courtney was wearing a black velvet dress, trimmed at the cuffs with lace. Brian was in the front, but Sage was clearly visible beside him. Her eyes widened and her warm expression dropped away and grew wooden for just a second. Gathering her composure quickly, she smiled a bright, meaningless smile although her eyes remained distant, cold.

'Brian, Sage. It's so nice to see you two together like this.'

Without apology Brian edged past the woman and into the living room, his eyes searching the interior of the house. Beryl nearly grabbed at his arm as he entered, but again managed to compose herself and gestured to Sage Paxton.

'Please come in.'

Sage, who knew that Brian's search of the house had been anything but idle, was surprised to hear his brother say, 'The place is looking just fine, Beryl. You'll have to let me give you a few dollars for the work you've done here.'

That seemed to shock Beryl more than seeing the two brothers together had. Brian offering her money for cleaning what she had taken as her own home — whoever she eventually shared it with — as if she were nothing more than hired help! Brian had his back turned toward them so that Sage could not read his expression, but he would have bet that his brother was smiling.

Sage could see no signs that dinner had been prepared; there was no scent of cooking in the air. Perhaps realizing this, Beryl fabricated excuses. 'I thought you two weren't coming. I thought there might have been some trouble in town that Brian had to take care of. It was getting so late.'

'This is the time you told us to get here,' Sage Paxton said. He was now almost certain that Brian's conjecture was correct. They had been invited not to supper but to their own execution. Beryl was smiling. It was the prettiest damn smile, innocent and caring.

'Can we at least have some coffee?' Brian asked. 'It was a long ride out here.'

'There's some on the stove,' Beryl said hastily. 'I'll get it.'

'Don't bother,' Brian said. He had already started that way. 'I'll do it.' Brian's hand dangled near his pistol. Sage knew that his brother wished to examine the rest of the house for lurking gunmen. He decided that his brother had become a pretty sharp lawman. Well then, at least one of them had profited from the past few years.

Sage eased past Beryl to follow, leaving the woman to sag on to the leather sofa as if the excitement of seeing the two Paxton brothers together had gotten to be too much for her. Perhaps it had.

Sage found Brian standing in the center of the room. He glanced at Sage and indicated the small kitchen table where two neat little cups of blue-painted white ceramic rested. Beryl had been expecting only one of them to return — if one of the two cups had not been intended for someone else entirely. Sage went to the small kitchen window beside the back door and drew back the curtain to look out into the night-darkened yard. Brian shook his head.

'The signal hasn't been given yet,' Brian said. Sage remembered that his brother was certain that there would be a signal given before the intended attack. Sage was not so sure, but a quick inspection of the shadowy yard revealed nothing.

'What do we do now?' Sage asked Brian.

'Pour us a cup of coffee, then we'll sit down and have a nice little chat with our hostess.'

'They won't wait long, Brian, she never planned on serving us supper.'

'No, someone's around somewhere — I can almost smell a skunk.'

'He has to be upstairs, doesn't he? I can't see anyone booting in the front door to come after us. Unless they were waiting for us to leave the house to attack.'

'That's too chancy in the dark,' Brian believed. 'Besides, I think that Beryl wants to watch it happen. She does like to be sure, as I've told you.'

'That's pretty dirty, for a woman.'

'Someone who doesn't mind burning two old folks in their bed is not the squeamish type.'

'I wonder if she locked the door to their room after setting the fire so that they couldn't get out,' Sage mused pointlessly.

'Did or didn't, it was a hellish way to commit murder . . . for a house and a piece of property. Let's not let her get lonely,' Brian said, splashing coffee into two heavy white mugs. He handed these to Sage and then filled one of the small cups on the table which he carried himself, placed on the low table in front of the sofa. Brian accepted one of the mugs from Sage, then turned again to face Beryl.

'There's still time to call it off, Beryl,' Brian said.

'I'm sure I don't know what you mean,' she responded, with that innocent little smile of hers. 'Call what off, Brian, the wedding, or . . . ?'

'Oh, hell, Beryl,' the voice said from the stairway and their heads turned to see Charlie Cable standing there, shotgun in his hands. 'It's over — they've figured it out.

'You, Marshal, and you, Sage, slide on over in the direction of the doorway, will you? I want to make as little mess as possible in my house. Beryl's getting a little tired of cleaning up.'

11

Neither brother was truly surprised at Charlie Cable's appearance. But his savage intent to shotgun them down in their own house was more than a little disconcerting.

In a steely voice, Brian Paxton said, 'The only messes Beryl needs to clean up around here are the ones she's made herself.' From the corner of his eyes, Sage could see the woman easing away from them.

'I didn't come here to talk,' Charlie Cable said, descending two more steps. Brian glanced at Sage and, without need for further communication, they threw themselves as far away from the twin muzzles of Cable's shotgun as possible, Sage rolling toward the front door while Brian flung himself to the floor behind the table resting in front of the sofa.

Charlie Cable's shotgun roared and belched flame. The table where Brian had dived was torn to splinters at this range. Sage had never stopped in his rolling and now came up behind the heavy leather chair which had been his father's, and with his Colt in his hand, blazed away at Cable through the smoke left behind by the shotgun blast.

He heard Cable grunt and the second load of buckshot was loosed in Sage's direction. Sage hid his head away again as the big old chair was torn to ribbons of leather and balls of white stuffing. Sage waited, counting to three, but Cable had decided against reloading the scattergun. He flung it at Sage then ran for the front door of the house, banging it open to the night.

Sage rose again, fired inaccurately at the fleeing Cable and simultaneously saw that Brian had not risen from his hiding place. 'Brian!'

'I'm all right,' Brian said, though it was plain to see that he had been struck in both arms and his chest by the shotgun pellets.

'Let me help you!' Beryl was screaming. 'Oh, Brian, let me help you!'

'All right,' Brian panted, getting to his feet with the aid of the table. 'You can help me, Beryl — by grabbing your coat and getting out of here. And don't ever come back, for any reason!'

Still panting, Brian sagged back on to the sofa, which was smoldering from the hot lead that had been poured into it. He took a quick look under his blue shirt, assessing the damage, and yelled at his brother:

'What are you doing standing there, Sage? Get after him!'

Feeling like a commanded soldier given his instructions, Sage Paxton turned sharply on his heel and followed Charlie Cable out into the dark of night. Behind him he could hear Beryl whimpering her innocence, her love, and the sharp rebuffing bark of his wounded brother.

Standing for a moment near his gray

horse Sage listened to the night whispers. He thought he could hear a horse racing away, its hoofs' racket muffled by the distance. 'Let's see how near to healthy you really are,' Sage said, swinging aboard the gray.

He turned the horse sharply away from the hitch rail and spurred it immediately into a full run. There was no moon in the sky, few stars to light his way, but Sage knew this route as well as any man alive and he raced on at the top of the horse's speed across the long grass valley, heedless of any obstacles.

After a while he forced himself to slow. It was that or run the big gray into the ground. Finally pulling his horse to a full stop, he patted the shuddering horse's neck and listened. He could hear no more of the horse which Cable had started in this direction, though Sage was sure that the man could not have gained ground on him, not the way he had been riding.

'Is he hiding out from us?' Sage asked the horse. Charlie Cable had proven himself to be quite capable of shooting from ambush. Would the bad man have given up his mad rush toward freedom to patiently set up among the trees and take his second chance to dry-gulch Sage? Not in this light, Sage decided, glancing toward the barely glimmering stars set in the blackness of the sky.

Sage started on again, a little more carefully. His initial mad dash after Cable had been prompted by the knowledge that the man had nearly taken his brother's life. Having only just on this day found his brother, remembered the sort of man Brian Paxton truly was, he had let anger take the reins of his pursuit.

Care and a reasonable speed was a better approach in his hunt for Charlie Cable. It bothered Sage a little that Cable had stopped, or at least slowed. Sage had figured the man for a race to Trinity. Possibly he still had associates there, but that seemed unlikely. The game was up now, and Charlie must know that. Where would he go?

Judge Cable's ranch was not likely. It seemed Cable had disowned his son, perhaps for antics like this. Brian had said that he had reports of Cable being involved in other dark business, the judge must have heard the rumors as well. A man of Judge Cable's stature would not have been able to stomach the idea that his son had gone bad, hit the outlaw trail.

Where then would Charlie go? Into Trinity, hoping to find help before Charlie Cable could be recognized by Deputy Harvey? That, too, seemed more unlikely the more Sage thought about it. That left . . .

Sage suddenly reined his horse to another halt, looking toward the eastern, forested hills. Someone had been staying there, Sage knew because of his last visit there with Gwen. Perhaps Charlie Cable had clothes there, loot from some of his earlier depredations, even another, fresh horse staked out among the trees.

It suddenly seemed more likely than not, and so Sage turned the gray horse toward the cabin in the pines.

With the exception of Brian, Sage Paxton knew those hills and their secret paths better than any man alive. Cable had likely not taken the time to explore the woods as Sage had when he was a boy. Why would he? Therefore, it was safe to assume that Charlie Cable knew only of the front road which ran directly to the cabin's door, and had no other plan in mind for escape but to use the same trail when he deemed the time right.

He would be watching that trail all the time he worked, gathering his possessions or saddling a new horse, maybe even be comforted by the fact that no one ever showed up on his heels. Cable would be constantly working, but constantly alert. But it would do him no good to keep watch. There were hundreds of ways to approach the cabin, and Sage Paxton now rode one of them.

The trees were close in the night, trying to crowd him from his trail. He passed the huge gray boulder that he had climbed as a kid. He could clamber up to its heights with relative ease, whereas Brian could not. It gave Sage a sense of superiority in those young years.

Emerging from the trees, he could see the home cabin. Behind the window a single dim light showed, a moving light as if someone were searching the place with a single candle, which Charlie Cable undoubtedly was doing, retrieving his gear and any stolen loot he might have hidden there.

Behind the house stood Cable's chestnut horse, looking weary and unhappy, though its ears perked at the sight of the gray horse Sage rode. Sage swung down from the saddle. And now what?

His choices were limited. He did not care for the notion of kicking in the door and blazing away in the night. Pausing only momentarily, he made his decision. Charlie would not remain long inside; he was in a hurry to depart the area. Sage decided to simply wait for him to emerge, hands probably full, burdened by whatever he had stowed in the cabin.

He slipped behind a huge twin-pine tree. Resisting the urge to sit and rest, he stood with his rifle at the ready. Charlie Cable, he thought, you might be a fine cattleman, and a great lover, but you're not too good at hide and seek.

Sage did not need to plumb the depths of his patience; within minutes he saw the dim light extinguished and a harried-looking Charlie Cable round the house in the deep darkness. Charlie pulled up short, dropping the gunny sack he had been toting in his right hand. He had seen a second horse standing beside his chestnut. Now he muttered, 'Who the hell . . . ?'

'You shouldn't even have to guess,

Charlie,' Sage Paxton's voice said from out of the depths of the black night. 'You should have taken more care with your planning. You shouldn't have stowed your goods here, but then again I guess you never figured on needing to retrieve them so soon.'

'Sage Paxton! Damn you,' Cable breathed.

'That's who, and I've got you in my sights, Charlie. If you shuck your guns I might even let you live, though it goes against the grain seeing as you shot my brother down.'

'Yeah,' Charlie answered with a sneer, 'I'm sure I'd get a fair trial in Trinity after shooting their marshal.' Sage knew that the man was stalling, trying to find Sage's figure in the night against the background of black trees.

'It's that or I gun you down where you stand,' Sage said, figuring that he was still giving Cable a better chance than he had given Brian Paxton.

'Oh, the hell with it! The hell with you,' Cable said, as he drew and fired.

His shots came remarkably close, plucking at the bark of the tree not a foot from Sage's head. It was close, but not close enough — Sage, who had kept his Winchester's sights trained on Charlie Cable, triggered off.

Cable dropped straight to the ground without a scream, a curse or a groan, and lay there as his startled chestnut horse sidestepped away from the fallen body. After taking a minute to be sure, Sage stepped forward from the trees. The sound of the echoing shots had died away to silence in the night. Working in that silence, Sage collected the possessions Cable had been carrying and tied them to the back of the chestnut. Harvey could sort through whatever was in there and return what stolen goods he could identify among them.

Cable's body he left on the earth where it lay. He felt no need to transport the remains to Trinity, nor could he stop now and take the time to bury him even if he had a shovel, which he did not. There was just no time.

There was still unfinished business to be taken care of on this cold night.

The temperature had dropped dramatically as Sage had expected it to as he trailed out of Trinity on the icy night. Cresting out the hills he spotted the tiny dark house which was now faintly illuminated by a rising crescent moon.

Harvey had been at the office when Sage had ridden in. After listening to Sage, he dropped the burlap sack on his desk and said, 'That's heavy enough. There might be something in there to help somebody out.' Harvey pushed away from his desk and stood, looking worried. 'I've got to get someone to rouse the doctor and send him out to your ranch. You think Brian is still all right?'

'I think he is — now. He might have to spend a day or two out at the house if you can handle things.'

'I can,' Harvey answered, before admitting, 'but everything is a lot easier for me when Brian is around. You wouldn't know this, Sage, but your brother is a good lawman and a well-respected one in this town. We'd hate like hell to lose him.'

Harvey was already in motion to find some help before Sage had stepped into leather once again. It was time to end things, to finally find the end of the long trail to Trinity . . .

* * *

The small house remained dark as Sage Paxton approached it on his now heavy-legged gray horse. The big animal had given Sage its all, and outside of its weary stride still showed no sign of the earlier damage to its leg.

Now, how to do this?

Sage was sitting on his horse, considering the best way to go about things. He didn't wish to startle the old ladies by banging on their door at this hour. As he swung down from his saddle, the door opened a few inches and then was filled by the slender form of Gwen Mackay, illuminated only by the high-riding moon, which sent pale rays of light against her nightgown-clad form. He walked toward her automatically, and without thinking of it, felt his arms go around her slender warmth to draw her near.

'I thought you might come back. I was watching for you.'

'Get your riding clothes,' Sage said in a whisper.

Stepping away, Gwen asked in an answering whisper, 'Why? Have you found another place for me to stay?'

'Do you like it here?'

'I like my aunts well enough, but I can tell I'm interfering with usual ways. They don't know exactly what is to be done with me.'

'I do,' Sage answered. They still were speaking in whispers. 'Get dressed. I'll outfit your horse.'

'Where're you taking me?' Gwen asked hesitantly. 'I won't be alone, will I? I don't like being alone, Sage.'

'You won't be alone,' Sage Paxton promised.

The girl scuttled into the house, moving silently in the darkness. Sage went to find and outfit the bay horse Mike Currant had unintentionally willed to her back along the Vasquez. Sage waited with the horses for only a few minutes. When Gwen exited it to clamber aboard her horse, still no light had been seen within.

'Did you tell them?' Sage asked as he mounted his gray.

'I didn't want to wake them up. I left a note on the kitchen table.'

'That's going to come as a shock,' Sage said, turning his horse to follow Gwen from the yard.

'Not much of one, I don't think. I think it'll ease their minds not to have to worry about me. I'll come back in a day or two to explain' — she paused — 'if that will be possible. I don't even know where you're taking me.'

'It's possible,' was all Sage said in reply.

They rode on in silence to the barren crest of the hill and started on once again toward Trinity.

'Well?' Gwen asked when they were near enough to town to see its lights. 'Where are you taking me, Sage?'

'First there's some business to be gotten out of the way,' Sage said, glancing skyward. 'I killed a man tonight. I have to go and tell his father, Judge Cable is his name, how it happened.'

'Sage, how terrible for you! And for his father.'

'Somehow I don't think it will be that much of a shock to Cable. He's been watching his son go bad for a long time. And,' Sage said, now looking directly into Gwen's eyes, 'there's another, private matter I need to talk to him about.'

'What's that?' Gwen asked curiously. A slight inkling of Sage's thinking caused a small smile to show at the corner of her mouth.

'I told you that his name is *Judge* Cable, didn't I?' Sage said, now looking away uneasily from the small woman at his side.

'I think I know what you're hinting at,' Gwen said. 'But if it's what I think — Sage, have you even asked the girl?'

'We haven't even gotten there yet,' Sage Paxton answered in a dry voice.

'And it don't look like you ever will,' a rough voice said from out of the darkness as a man appeared on the trail ahead of them from behind a patch of high-growing sumac.

Austin Szabo, rifle at the ready, rode directly toward them, halted the fancy black horse he was riding and said, 'I'll have my woman back now, Paxton.'

12

Sage sat his gray horse, finding he was shivering a little. From what he knew about Austin Szabo, there was little doubt that the man would shoot if it seemed called for. With another man, Sage would have talked, bargained for time, but Szabo's steely glare was fixed on Sage, measuring the position of his gun, gauging his intent.

'I said I will have my woman, Paxton. You just ride along and maybe you'll live to see the sunrise.'

Sage still had not decided on a tactic — if there was one possible. At his side a defiant Gwen Mackay shrieked, 'I'm not your woman and you'll never have me!' At the same time she slapped heels to the flanks of her bay horse and the startled animal bolted ahead. At its first leap, Szabo stretched out an arm to grab the horse's bridle. It was just enough of a move, just enough of a distraction for Sage to draw his Colt and fire point blank, without remorse or the time for it, into Szabo's neck. It was a close shot, but all that was needed as Szabo's own black reared up and dropped the dead outlaw to the ground from its back.

Gwen brought her pony under control and backed it to halt beside Sage, who had swung down to examine Szabo's body.

'Is he dead?' she asked a little shakily, as Sage stood, dusting his hands together.

'He gives every indication of being so,' Sage said through dry lips. 'And not a single person on earth to care or mourn him.'

'Why would anyone even bother — the sort of man he was? Sage, can we ride away from him?'

'That's a fine idea,' Sage Paxton said in a low voice. He swung aboard his horse again. The long trail to Trinity had finally ended — hadn't it? There was no one left to hate; no one to kill. He wondered briefly if it had all been worth it, but then he glanced at the dark-eyed woman riding beside him, a wavering smile on her face, and he knew that it had been. He would ride through hell for Gwen.

'Now you'll have to report two dead men to the judge,' Gwen said, as they reached Trinity, circled it toward where Sage knew Judge Cable's modest house stood. Sage was briefly thoughtful.

'I've considered that, but, no, I think I'll just let Austin Szabo's death go unremarked in every way. If I change my mind, I'll talk to Harvey, or to my brother.'

The judge, wearing a nightshirt tucked into his trousers, answered the door himself as if he had been waiting for some night visitor. Leading them inside, he asked, 'It's Charlie, isn't it?'

'I'm afraid so,' Sage had to tell him as they entered a room bright with firelight. He saw the expression on Judge Cable's face; it was only rueful.

'I told Charlie all of his life to avoid bad company, but I never thought the one to do him in would be wearing satin and lace. That's the way it was, wasn't it?'

'Just about,' Sage answered. 'I'll tell you about it, if you like.'

'He tried to kill Brian Paxton!' the judge said when Sage was almost finished with his tale. It was the only time during their visit that the judge showed any real emotion. For the most part Cable had only stood, wagging his head heavily, staring into the fire.

The story seemed short in the re-telling. Sage fell silent. He did notice Gwen glancing at him to see if perhaps Sage had changed his mind and would continue, to tell the judge about the death of Austin Szabo. When he did not, figuring Cable had received enough troublesome news for one night, she was obviously relieved.

'Will Brian be all right?' the judge asked, still studying the curling flames in the fireplace.

'He was when I left. Harvey was going to send some men out to check on him.'

'Why did you leave?' Judge Cable wondered. Sage laughed briefly. 'It was Brian's command. He gave me an order like I was one of his deputies, and I just automatically obeyed.'

'Yes — Brian Paxton can be a forceful man, the kind of marshal that Trinity needs. I wish him a full recovery. The one thing you have not told me,' the judge said, leveling probing eyes on Sage Paxton's, 'is how this young woman came to be riding with you.'

Of course Cable had seen the looks the two had been exchanging throughout their visit; they were not new ones to the judge. He had been in the business for a long time. Cable waved off the explanation he did not really need to hear and went to his desk for his marrying book.

★   ★   ★

208

Beryl was long gone from the ranch, but Brian Paxton remained there, sporting fresh bandages. 'I wanted to wait around and see how you'd fared,' he said to his brother. 'Charlie Cable could be foxy.'

'Greed sealed his fate,' Sage said, settling on the wounded leather sofa with Gwen close beside him, her eyes sparkling. 'Charlie Cable couldn't bring himself to simply ride out leaving a sackful of loot behind.'

Sage again rolled out his story as Brian sat facing them, his eyes asking more questions than his mouth. Gwen met his gaze, blushed and turned her eyes away in embarrassment. Sage had reached the point of the meeting with Judge Cable when Brian held up a hand and asked the same question Cable had asked. Sage answered.

'Well, since I knew that Harvey was sending out some men to look after you, I figured I had time to stop and pick up a bride before returning.'

Brian looked at Gwen once again,

standing though it obviously caused him discomfort, and shook his brother's hand. 'Congratulations, Sage. You definitely do have your mysterious ways, but they seem to have worked this time. She's a lovely girl. You'll have to tell me all about how you did it sometime.' Looking around, Brian then said, 'As long as I'm on my feet, I'd just as well be going.'

'That's liable to be too much riding for you, Brian.'

'I'll make it all right. If I leave now I'll just be about on time to drop by the doctor's and have my regular restaurant breakfast. Then I'll let Harvey have the job for the rest of the day.'

They stood and watched as Brian, hobbling quite a bit, placed his hat on his head and started out toward his horse in the first gray predawn light. Sage watched his brother mount his leggy bay horse awkwardly, lifted a hand in farewell, then latched the door shut.

'I don't think we should have let him

go alone,' Gwen said, as Sage returned to hold her in his arms.

'He didn't want us along. He wanted us to stay here together. I wasn't about to challenge his ability to ride or refuse an offered gift. If he feels he can't make it, he'll stop at the old cabin.

'As for us — I'm not anxious to see that town again anytime soon. It'll be a while before I'm ready to ride that trail to Trinity again.'

They went off to bed then as the sky outside brightened with a flourish of color. It had been a long night but promised to be a fine morning.

A FINAL SHOOT-OUT

J. D. Kincaid

When Abe Fletcher is released from prison, he's anxious to reclaim his inheritance — a beautiful and flourishing ranch. At the same time, bank robbers Red Ned Davis and Hank Jolley are fleeing from justice and holed up with Jolley's cousin, Vic Morgan. After a chance encounter between Abe and Vic, the outlaws agree to help Abe regain his inheritance — for a price. However, their plans go awry due to the unexpected intervention of a seductive saloon singer, Arizona Audrey, and the famous Kentuckian gunfighter, Jack Stone . . .

SCATTERGUN SMITH

Max Gunn

When Scattergun Smith sets out after the infamous outlaw Bradley Black, his search leads him across dangerous terrain, and every fibre of his being tells him that he is travelling headfirst into the jaws of trouble. But Black has both wronged the youngster Smith and killed innocent people, and has to pay. Scattergun is determined to catch and end the life of the ruthless outlaw before Black claims fresh victims. It will take every ounce of his renowned expertise to stop him, and prove why he is called Scattergun Smith.

CROSSROADS

Logan Winters

When a wealthy rancher mistakes K. John Landis and a cantankerous ex-saloon girl for an honourable couple and offers them the opportunity to make some much-needed money, the pair jump at the chance. In charge of the rancher's flighty daughter, and playing the role of doting husband, Landis is dragged down into the violent underworld of Crossroads. He had feared leaving town without a nickel in his jeans — now he fears he might never leave again . . .

THE MAN FROM JERUSALEM

Jack Martin

Day after day, the sun does its utmost to roast the very land upon which the dilapidated town of Jerusalem sits. Johnny Jerusalem is returning home to the town of his namesake. He'd left years ago, but no sooner is he back than the little money he has is stolen from him during a bank robbery. He sets out with a young gunslinger to find the culprits who have wronged him — but there's a posse behind them, and bandits ahead of them, and soon the bullets are flying . . .

THE APPLEJACK MEN

Caleb Rand

Ruben Byrd is wrongly arrested for acts of treachery. To prove his innocence and find the men responsible, he has to break out of military prison. But when he eventually catches up with his target, he realizes that things have changed . . . In the town of Vinegar Wells, the sheriff proposes a two-day bail for the real turncoats to be brought to book, and Ruben has little choice but to accept. With a suspicious quarry in front of him and grasping hunters behind, however, he finds himself in a perilous situation . . .

GHOST TOWN

Roy Patterson

Clint Shane and his pal Ty Morrow think they have found a settlement where they can rest and buy fresh provisions. But as they ride towards the sprawling town, suddenly shots ring out. Terrified, they spur their mounts and gallop across the wild terrain towards the array of buildings that are bathed in the blinding sunlight. Soon, however, they find that this is no ordinary town; there are no people. As more shots ring out, Morrow and Shane realize they have taken refuge in a ghost town . . .

THE
BOX
OF
DEMONS

Daniel Whelan was born in Cheshire, but grew up in North Wales. He moved to London in 2000 to study for a degree in Acting. His adaptation of Richard Adams's *Watership Down* premiered at Riverside Studios and was acclaimed by Mr Adams as one of the best he'd read. His next play, *A Harlot's Progress*, inspired by the etchings of Hogarth, was well received by *Time Out*. Alas, Mr Hogarth was too dead to give his opinion.